FREEDOM'S EDGE

An American Trilogy

A Story of America's War for Independence in the South:
The People Who Fought and Won, and Those Who Fought and Lost

Jill LaForge Jones

Book One
ESCAPING YESTERDAY

Also by the Author

Written as Jill Jones:
Emily's Secret
My Lady Caroline
The Scottish Rose
Essence of My Desire (retitled A Scent of Magic)
Circle of the Lily
The Island
Bloodline
Remember Your Lies
Every Move You Make

Written as Emily LaForge:
Beneath the Ravens' Moon
Shadow Haven

AUTHOR BIO

Jill LaForge Jones is the award-winning author of eleven novels of romance and suspense. She holds a bachelor's degree in Journalism with emphasis on Professional Writing from the University of Oklahoma where she graduated Magna Cum Laude and was inducted into Phi Beta Kappa. She has written for a wide variety of audiences and media, including print, audio, video, and online content. During the last twenty years, she served as director of the Swannanoa Valley Museum in Black Mountain, NC, and director of Marketing & Communications for the Blue Ridge National Heritage Area, work in which she traveled throughout the region and learned about the unique history and culture of western North Carolina.

AUTHOR'S NOTE

When I was growing up, the history taught in school about America's war for independence was generally depicted through a lens of northern action—the Boston Tea Party, Lexington and Concord, Paul Revere's midnight ride, creation of the Declaration of Independence in Philadelphia, George Washington and Valley Forge, etc. As a student, I was given the impression that the whole thing was relatively simple, based on the "taxation without representation" issue, freedom of religion, and the desire of early immigrants for affordable land.

While all this is true, the picture is far more complex, and it leaves out entire cultures of the natives of the land who were not only disenfranchised by the white man's encroachment, but also came perilously close to extinction. It leaves out the story of the immigrants who forged their new lives in the South—primarily South and North Carolina—and who played a significant role in the eventual defeat of Cornwallis. And it fails to depict the complexity of the relations between white and red man, between a culture with superior technology and one still in the stone age (think guns vs. bow and arrow, steel knives vs. stone spear points.) The story fails to show how over time, the natives' desire to own that technology, partly in self-defense, and to trade with the British for their weapons, manufactured goods, and even trinkets led them to concede land through treaties that many times were ignored or broken. In spite of this, the Cherokee were allies of the British in the War for Independence, and as such met defeat as well.

As a twenty-first century white female, it is difficult to imagine life on this southern frontier between 1750-1780. Who were these immigrants who came into places like Charleston and Wilmington rather than the more typical points of entry such as Philadelphia and New York? Why did they come? What were they running to? Or from? Did they come of their own accord, or were they indentured or enslaved? How bad was life where they came from that they would risk everything and face the unknown in a land rich with promise but rife with danger?

And what of those who already lived on that land? Natives whose ancestors had been there for thousands of years? What did they make of these newcomers? And what part did they play in the white man's war for independence?

Immigration and the problems inherent in the process have been part of the history of mankind since the beginning of time: One tribe wants the land of another, and so will take it by force or cunning. Or one tribe builds a wall to keep another tribe from entering its land. Or tribes unite through marriage or treaty only to fall apart again through treachery or betrayal. It is a never-ending saga of humankind.

My quest is not to resolve this eternal issue, but rather through this work of historical fiction provide the reader with insight into the incredible complexities that faced both the immigrants who came into the southern ports of the British colonies in the mid-eighteenth century and the natives already upon these shores. I have tried to remain true to historic dates and figures, but this is fiction, life imagined in a time and place over two and a half centuries ago, and history sometimes gets fuzzy—in my research, I sometimes encountered different versions of events, times, and places. I have chosen the ones that best fit my story.

My "tribes" are primarily the British, Irish, Highland Scots, Africans, and the Cherokee, descendants of all of which can be found in the mountains and valleys of western North and South Carolina and northern Georgia today. Other "contributing tribes" include the French, Moravians, Scots-Irish, Germans, Swiss, and the Catawba, Shawnee and Creek Indians. The mountains and foothills of North and South Carolina became home to a stew of humanity from both sides of the Atlantic and both hemispheres, brought together by hope, despair, fear, greed, desire for power, lust for land, and that ultimate and elusive aspiration, freedom.

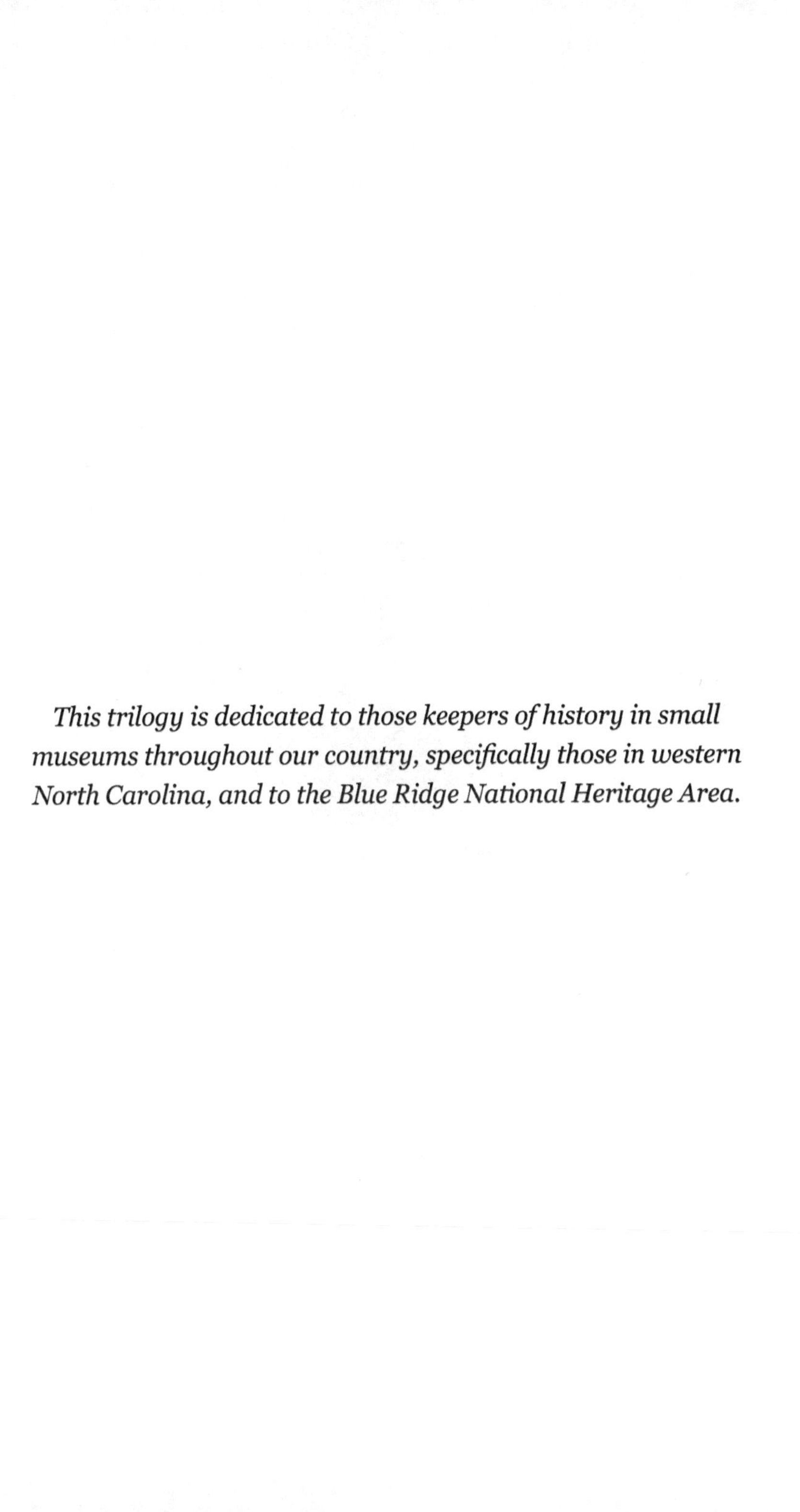

This trilogy is dedicated to those keepers of history in small museums throughout our country, specifically those in western North Carolina, and to the Blue Ridge National Heritage Area.

Chapter One

Northern Ireland, May 1751

A chill spring wind rattled the fragile windowpanes, and dark clouds scudded over the barren hills, spitting rain. From the single window in the tiny cottage, Fiona Cassidy kept an eye on the road, anxious for the return of her father from the market in Derry. Since early this morning, she'd been filled with a sense of dread, and the storm did nothing to ease her mind.

Something terrible had happened in Derry. She was certain of it. Her special senses— what her Granny called the Sight—told her so.

When at last she saw him approaching along the dirt road, his demeanor was all wrong.

Normally standing tall, a proud man in spite of his poverty, today his head was bowed as he pushed the market wagon before him. Had he been robbed of the pitiful load of winter vegetables he'd gone there to sell? Had he been beaten?

She dashed out the door to help him bring the heavy wagon to the house. "Da?" she cried over the rush of the wind. "Are ye all right?" She saw his eyes were red, tear-swollen. "What's happened? What's wrong, Da?"

He just shook his head and nodded toward the door and the warmth of the cottage, where a meager peat fire burned in the small hearth. She helped him remove his threadbare woolen coat and made tea, not pushing him further for answers. He would speak when he was ready, she knew. And not until then.

He nodded as she set the tin cup before him but remained silent. He took a few sips, then spoke quietly. "I have made the hardest decision of my life," he said at last, his voice hoarse. He took another swallow. "I have bought ye passage to America."

It took a moment for his words to register with Fiona. "You have done what?"

Aidan Cassidy drew in a deep breath and looked his daughter straight in the eye. "I have made arrangements with a ship's captain to take you to America, where you'll have a good job and eventually be free."

Fiona stared at her father in disbelief. "Arrangements? What kind of arrangements?"

Aidan hesitated, then replied, "It's called an indenture. I have made arrangements for your passage to America in exchange for your servitude to a family who lives in Charlestown. The family will reimburse the captain for your passage. When you have completed the terms of the contract, you will be free."

Astounded, Fiona was at first speechless, then she managed, "Servitude! You mean you have sold me? Sold me like a cow?"

"It's not like that, Fiona. I did not sell you; I found a way to buy your passage to America. I'm sorry you're so unhappy about this," her father said sharply. "I thought perhaps you would look at it differently, for the chance to have a better life in a better place. That's why I did it, and now there's no goin' back. I'm to take you to Derry on the morrow."

"The morrow!" Fiona was aghast and thought for a moment she would be sick. Instead, she allowed tears to spill down her cheeks. "I don't understand why you are shipping me off to some godforsaken unknown place," she murmured, wondering what she'd done to deserve this.

Aidan's face softened, and he attempted a smile. "It's not exactly unknown, Fiona. Nor is it godforsaken. It's America. The New World. A place where you will get a new start, have a new life, hope..." he broke off, and Fiona suddenly realized what had been missing in her father for some time now.

Hope.

She saw him in a new light just then, saw him for what he was, a broken man, beaten down by life, hopeless. He'd been different before, fun-loving and most times happy in spite of their hard lives as tenant farmers on the harsh, poorly productive land on which they lived. But before, when he was down, he'd bring out his fiddle and sing some lively tunes with his wife and children, and for a while, even for a night, hold the world at bay.

And then came the pox. First her sister, Maureen, then little brother Daniel, and then their beautiful mother, Maura. Many died that year as the pestilence swept the countryside, taking hundreds to their graves. Fiona often felt guilty that somehow, she had been spared. Only she, her father, and Granny were left in their entire family. The rest of their family, indeed their small *clachan*, their village, had been decimated by that pestilence.

Granny! Fiona's mind raced. The old woman lived alone up in the hills and kept to the old ways. Granny was a wise woman, a seer, a healer, a fine spinner of flax; some said her threads were made from magic. She'd taught Fiona many things, including spinning, but most importantly, always to question. "Does Granny know you planned to do this?" Fiona suddenly thought perhaps she could run away to Granny's until the ship left Derry without her.

"She doesn't know, and yet...well, she does," her father replied, his voice raspy. "You know how she is; she knows things. She's coming now; I can feel her near."

It came as no surprise that Granny would know about this and would come to her. What surprised her was that her father sensed it too. Did he have the Sight? She'd always thought it came to her through Granny and then Ma.

"I hope so, Da." Her voice softened. "I must see her. There is so much to say before...if...I go."

"I understand," Aidan replied. "But ye will go. There's no 'if' to it. This grieves me beyond words, Fiona," he added, standing to leave. "Believe that. I wouldn't a-done it if I didn't think it was for your best, and I think your Granny will agree." With that, he turned and left the cottage, shutting the door behind him with a bang.

Chapter Two

After he left, Fiona sat alone in the dimness of their small hut, the room lit only by the daylight that struggled through the tiny window and the glow of the fire in the hearth. A thousand thoughts and feelings raged through her. First, how could he do this to her? She was fourteen, would be fifteen next winter, almost a grown woman. It should be her choice.

In the heat of their argument, he'd mentioned something about the English threatening to take all the young, able-bodied Irish to work on sugar cane plantations in the Caribbean. "They have big plantations there, and they need workers. Strong workers like the Irish," he'd said, his tone turning bitter. "They'll take you, Fiona, trust my word. And it won't be the same as here. No tenant farming."

"What then?"

He paused, then replied, looking straight at her. "Slavery, pure and simple. You wouldn't get paid, nor be able to farm your own food." He swallowed hard, then added, "They say it's better to move valuable workers there than to leave them here to starve."

Slavery. She pondered the word. He'd told her she would have to serve, unpaid, as a lady's maid to the wife of a wealthy Englishman. How did that differ from slavery? What would guarantee her freedom at the end of the agreement?

Charlestown! A lady's maid! It was beyond her comprehension. And what lay between here and there? An ocean voyage. What would the captain be like? What would she do on board those long days? She'd heard the passage could take months. Would she be sick? Would there be food? What if she died before they reached the New World?

Fiona was building up a mountain of fear when the door to the rough cottage opened again, and her Granny shuffled inside, toting a plaid woolen satchel that she lowered to the hard dirt floor. Fiona ran to her, flinging herself into the old woman's arms. "Oh, Granny, thank the gods you've come!"

"There, there, my child," Granny said, smoothing Fiona's rough red curls. "I saw what was happenin', and I knew ye needed me."

Fiona trusted her father to tell her the truth, but still she asked, "Did Da tell you his plans?"

Granny took Fiona by both arms and held her away so she could look into her face. "No. Your Da did this of his own accord. Out of love for ye, Fiona. It's been heavy on his mind for months."

"But he never spoke of it to you?" Fiona sniffed and led her grandmother to the table.

"He didna have to, child. You know that, and so does he."

"But why didn't you tell me? Warn me?"

"'Twasn't my place to meddle. And besides, I know he is right."

Fiona took her Granny's cloak and saw the fatigue on the old face. It was a fair journey from her place in the hills to Fiona's family's cottage. "I'll make us some tea," she said, filling the kettle again and setting it on the fire. "It's a long walk. You must be tired."

The old woman was silent for a long while. "Tea," she said at last. "Yes, that will be a good place to start."

Over tea and oat cakes, Granny began to tell Fiona what she knew. "I have voices that come to me, as ye know, child," she said. "I've heard many recently speaking of this plan of the English to carry away the children of Ireland. 'Tis an evil plan for sure, but one I know is already afoot. Your Da has managed to spare ye this sorrow. Ye mustn't be sad, or afraid."

"I am both," Fiona replied, feeling miserable but allowing the idea at last to enter her mind. "What's to become of me?" she asked almost in a whisper and drained her teacup.

Granny reached for it. "Let's see if we can find an answer here." Fiona had witnessed her Granny reading the tea leaves for others and knew she used them to focus her powerful, seemingly magical mind. Granny was the wise woman in this part of Ireland, and the country people sought her out for all kinds of advice. She was the one who brought babies into this world, and when the Christian priests weren't aware, also helped send the spirits of the dead into the netherworld with rituals older than time. She knew the secrets of the forest and field, what plant would heal, what plant would kill. These secrets she kept in a small book, and she'd shared many of them with Fiona. From her, Fiona had learned how to brew certain healing teas, create ointments, and even had assisted in childbirth. Granny had assured Fiona that one day, she, too, would be a wise woman. She had the Sight, Granny said. All she needed was to practice, and she could develop it.

Now, huddled over the metal teacup, Granny swirled the leaves and peered intently at them. "Humm," was all she uttered. And then, "Oh!"

"What? What is it, Gran?"

The old woman looked up, raised her eyebrows, and pushed the cup over to Fiona. "Look for yourself, child," she said. "Use your Sight. Tell me what ye see here."

Fiona's hand trembled as she took the cup. She'd practiced this art only a few times, and she wasn't totally sure she believed in it. Still, she believed in her Granny. She swirled the bit of liquid that was left, swishing the leaves along the sides of the cup. Some remained at the bottom. She stared hard and tried to clear her troubled mind. Slowly, to her astonishment, she saw, or rather felt, a hot place. She sensed rather than saw a journey. But then suddenly it wasn't one journey that came to her. It was many. And there were many people along the way. Strangers.

And strange beings, it seemed. So different. Some of them evil. A chill ran through her, and she shoved the cup away.

"Nay! I do not like what I see," she uttered.

"I saw them too, Fiona. The journeys. There's more coming to you than this ocean voyage. You must be brave as you travel them all, because you will be needed."

Fiona raised her head and frowned. "Needed?"

Granny reached down and brought the satchel to the table. "Yes. Needed. Ye know our ways. Ye know healing. Ye are strong and healthy yourself. 'Tis why ye were spared the pox." Out of the bag she drew several small boxes and two glass vials that Fiona recognized from her grandmother's herbal kitchen. "I brought these to get ye started," Granny said as if speaking to an apprentice. Which, Fiona guessed, she had been all along. She just hadn't thought of her training in that way.

Next came the small book that contained all of Granny's wisdom written down in the old language, the one Fiona had learned to read despite the law forbidding it. Her schooling was limited, but she could read some English as well. "Your book!" she exclaimed. "No, you can't do without that, Granny."

Her grandmother smiled kindly. "I haven't used that book in years, Fiona. It's all up here." She touched her head. "Trust me, ye will need this far more than I. It will help you along your way." Reluctantly Fiona accepted the small, worn book, swallowing hard over the tightness in her throat.

Granny delved into the satchel again and brought out a second small book and a long feather. "Fresh, for ye to keep your own notes," she said, pushing the book across the table. "There's ink in one of those bottles, and here's a quill."

"But how...where did you get this?" Fiona asked, fingering the thin pages.

"It's flax paper. Ye can make paper out of many things. Secret to making it is in the old book." She raised one eyebrow and gave a small smile. "Ye must always keep a book of spells, child. Ye can make another if ye run out of space in this'n."

From this seemingly bottomless bag, she next drew out a length of homespun linen cloth. "Ye'll need a new garment, and we haven't time to sew it tonight. So, take this cloth, and these," she handed over the fabric and a small pair of scissors, "and these." Two needles pierced a small piece of the cloth. "And this." Next came a ball of thread. "Ye can fashion the cloth using your dress as an example."

Before Fiona could say a word, her Granny went on. "There's one more thing," she said, "then we must put your travel things together, for ye must leave at first light." With that, she brought out a small pouch from which she produced a round, flat stone, slender and about half the size around than the teacup. In the fading light, she peered at it. "'Tis an ancient talisman, handed to me by my own granny, who received it from her own. It brings good luck and safety to the bearer, those whose powers are used for good. I've kept it near for protection when visiting the sick and birthing the new babes. I could have shared it with ye before now, but I knew the time wasn't yet right." She handed the stone and the pouch to Fiona. "That time is now."

Fiona thought she knew her Granny well, but she'd never seen this object. She bent toward the firelight to get a better look. The stone itself was plain, not a gemstone or a crystal. Carved into it were intersecting half circles connected by one full circle. Fiona was well aware of the many Celtic and Druidic stones and their carvings that dotted the Irish countryside, and she recognized the symbols.

Holding the talisman in the palm of her hand, she felt it grow warm, probably just from the heat of her own body, but somehow, it brought Fiona great comfort. She would be taking part of her home with her, her Ireland, and her Granny. "Thank you," she whispered.

"The satchel is for ye, too," her Granny said. "My dear husband, rest his soul, made it for me before ye were born. I'm not going anywhere, and I've given its contents to ye, so I won't be needing it any longer."

The two remained silent for a long while as the sun dipped and the gray sky deepened into the black of night. At length, Granny cleared her throat and stood. "Now, girl, let's get ye together for your new life. It's just past Beltane, you know, a time for new beginnings."

Chapter Three

The following morning, Granny was gone. Before Fiona had cried herself to sleep, she'd shared her last evening with the few remaining neighbors Aidan had invited over to bid her farewell. These gatherings were commonly known as American wakes because as loved ones left for the shores of America, it was unlikely they would ever return. Those left behind grieved as much as if their departing kin and friends were dead.

Aidan had brought out his fiddle, as he'd done in better times. Several neighbors had brought along instruments of their own, and the *ceilidh* began. Everyone sang, and someone passed around a bottle of liquor. The music eased Fiona's thoughts, and for a while, she forgot her fears and joined in the merriment. She even did her favorite high stepping dance, although her soft shoe made no sound on the smooth earthen floor of the cottage.

She hadn't noticed when her Granny had silently slipped out, headed home through the dark night. Only in the morning did she see the note scribbled on a page torn from the new notebook: "I want no part of tearful farewells. Love and spirit go with you always. Gran."

***

Fiona set out at dawn with her Da carrying the woolen satchel containing everything she owned. The journey to Derry would take a good part of the day if they walked at a steady pace. When they reached a rise after which her home would no longer be visible, she stopped and turned around. Her village looked tiny: small white cottages soiled and worn from the harsh weather, huddled together against a brown background that had yet to green up from winter. The smoke rising from the chimneys was thin and pale, as if it was as tired as the houses, as tired as the land. Seeing it from a new perspective, it appeared suddenly sad and forlorn.

Fiona batted away tears, turned her back to her home, and straightened. *You must be brave...you will be needed.* "I'm ready now, Da." Inside her pocket, she clenched her fingers around the talisman stone.

Derry was a bustling seaport with strong walls built long ago for protection from invasion. Fiona had only been there a few times, even though it wasn't far from their farm. The locals still called it Derry although, as with everything else, the English had claimed it and changed the name to Londonderry.

The ship that awaited Fiona was the *Lady Caroline*, a small trading vessel sailing under the English flag. Her Da told her the captain was headed to Liverpool to deliver his cargo of rum, sugar and cotton from the New World before returning to Charlestown. He'd made an emergency stop in Derry to repair damage sustained in a storm and to take on a few supplies before completing his commercial voyage.

It was food grown on the Cassidy tenant farm that caused her Da to encounter Captain John Michael. Aidan Cassidy was usually a law-abiding man, but hard times and desperation had compelled him to try to sell on the side some of what he grew for the English landlord, a forbidden practice. He'd traveled to Derry with a small cart carrying what was left of last year's potatoes, winter-grown turnips, new spring greens, and dried beans. At the dock, he'd seen the English trading captain and approached to see if he would buy the food.

Captain John Michael seemed an amiable character, Aidan related to Fiona on their walk. And he needed the food, so the deal was sealed, and Aidan received actual money in exchange. They'd repaired to a local pub, where over a pint the captain explained his ship's dilemma—it was a small trading vessel, and he was hoping the ship owner in Liverpool who hired him as his captain would provide a larger vessel soon, so his profits would be better. Over the second pint, he mentioned casually that he was looking for a good, healthy young woman to return to Charlestown with him, as he had a client there in need of a lady's maid for his wife.

And so, another deal was struck.

The docks were busy when they arrived late in the day, and Fiona was hungry. Her father took them to the same pub for a meal, and there they found Captain Michael.

"Ah, Cassidy, you've come then. I wondered if you'd changed your mind," he said, eyeing Fiona candidly. "So, this is the lass, aye?"

"'Tis my daughter, Fiona," Aidan said.

Captain Michael's eyes took careful measure of her, then he smiled. "Ah, yes, I'm sure she will do fine. Please, join me," he invited and drew out a chair, indicating for Fiona to sit.

Fiona took her seat, eyeing him warily. His smile seemed warm and genuine, but his face was flushed, and his eyes a bit too bright. She saw his glass was nearly empty, and a wave of trepidation washed through her.

The trepidation didn't appease her hunger, however, and she quickly downed the savory pie and small cup of ale her father bought for her. She scarcely paid attention to the adults' conversation as she ate, hearing tidbits about trade and shipping. But suddenly the captain asked, "Can she cook?" and Fiona's head jerked up.

"Of course, I can cook," she said, thinking him a fool. "I've been cooking since I was a wee girl."

The captain laughed. "Then you'll have a job aboard ship since my own cook just took off. Nowhere to be found, the scoundrel." Then he added, "Just for the leg of the journey from here to Liverpool. I'll pick up a cook there."

Aidan frowned. "I suppose that would do," he hedged, glancing at Fiona. "But that wasn't part of our original agreement, Captain."

The captain sized up the older man. "No, I suppose it wasn't. But I need a cook, and I would think a bright young lass such as she would get bored on this journey without something to occupy her."

Fiona glared at him. "Stop talking as if I wasn't here," she snapped. "If you need a cook, I'll cook for you. But," she added as an afterthought, "you need to pay my Da for that."

Both men sat back in surprise, and then the captain laughed. "Spirited lass, are ye?" He called for another pint, then said, "Very well, I shall do that, provided once on board, you will follow the captain's orders, just like everyone else on the crew. No sassing back."

Fiona ignored his last demand. The crew! She hadn't thought

about that. "Uh, how many are there," she asked, "on the crew?"

"'Tis a small ship. We usually sail with thirty-five, but we lost several on this voyage. Down to seventeen men until we get to Liverpool," he replied. "We'll recruit more hands there. But for now, it's what's on board, and with you and me, that makes nineteen to feed."

Fiona drew in a quick breath. Nineteen! The most she'd ever cooked for was her small family, and sometimes a meal for others on a festive occasion, but even then, she'd been part of a larger group preparing the food together. Good Lord, what was she getting into! Thank goodness the captain would recruit a real cook in Liverpool.

After they had eaten, Captain Michael took Fiona and her father out to the ship that was anchored in the River Foyle to get her settled in, as they were to set sail on the morning tide.

Fiona was used to living in the small, dark space of their cottage, but she found her new quarters confining, consisting of a tiny compartment with only a narrow bunk and no windows. The door had a sliding latch, which gave her some measure of comfort, as the sailors she'd seen as they came aboard appeared a fearsome lot.

Her quarters were towards the front of the ship, just off the galley where she was to cook.

The galley had a small iron stove and oven, with pots and kettles better than she'd known at home. Swinging from nets around the galley were provisions of potatoes, (had they come from the Cassidy farm?) turnips, and other stores. She was suddenly overwhelmed. How could she possibly cook for all these men by herself?

As darkness fell, the captain left them alone to say their farewells. "Ye'll be all right," her father assured her, holding her close and kissing the top of her head. "Just stay strong and keep that talisman Granny gave you close at hand."

Fiona's throat was so tight she couldn't reply, so she just nodded.

"I've something else for you," Aidan added, drawing away. He had brought with him a bag that Fiona assumed contained the few provisions for their long walk, and maybe some produce to try to sell in Derry. But to her surprise, he drew out his old fiddle, small and well-worn from decades of use. "You know how to play it. You've a fine ear, and you know our old tunes. It will remind you of home, and of...our... happy times together." Here he broke off and wiped his eye.

"Da, I can't take this. It's..." She started to say, "all you have left," and then she realized how incredibly, sadly true that was.

Aidan Cassidy placed the neck of the instrument in Fiona's hand and wrapped her fingers around it tightly. "It goes with you, girl, and with it, a part of me." With that, he bent and kissed her cheek, looked into her eyes and studied her face a long while, as if memorizing every detail. And then he turned away. "Godspeed," he said, his voice barely audible. And then he was gone.

CHAPTER FOUR

Fiona held her Da's fiddle close when she lay down in her cramped bunk after he left, but she slept little that night, unsure about anything in her life. At first, she was tempted to find a way off the ship and run back to the farm. But her Da's parting gift of the fiddle warned her not to take lightly the other gift he'd given her—a chance for a new life in a better place.

At last, just before dawn, she gave up and donned her dress, ran a comb through her unruly red hair and tied it behind her neck with a ribbon. She stood at the doorway of her tiny cubicle, one hand on the talisman in her pocket, the other on the latch, gathering courage to meet the day. She left her quarters and made her way onto the deck just as the sun peeked over the horizon. Standing at the railing, she looked out across the river toward the docks and saw that the wharf was already alive with the bustle of a busy seaport. She felt more than heard a presence behind her and wheeled about in alarm.

"Ah, girl, I didn't mean to scaire ye." The man spoke with a heavy accent, and his words came out on a breath that reeked of hard drink. Fiona took a step back.

"I...I'm not scared," she lied.

"Ye must be the lass the captain told us about," he wheezed and spit over the side of the ship. "One's going to Charlestown." He winked at her and grinned, showing a mouth with many teeth missing. "He says you're the new cook. So, what vittles are ye plannin' on this mornin'?"

It hadn't occurred to Fiona that her duties were to start immediately. "Uh, well, what do you usually have in the morning?"

The man wheezed a laugh. "Why, tea and cakes, blimey," he said mockingly, looking at her like she had two heads. He shook his own head, then turned and disappeared down the companionway to the fo'c'sle, muttering something to the effect that she'd never make it as the ship's cook.

Tea and cakes, blimey, my foot! Fiona thought crossly. She knew the man was making fun of her. But then, she had no idea what sailors ate for breakfast. Or any other meal for that matter. Maybe they did have tea and cakes.

Blimey! She needed to find Captain Michael. She made her way back to the galley, and to her great relief, she found the captain there. "Good morning, sir," she said.

"About damned time you showed up," Captain Michael snarled. Gone was the amicable man of the night before. Fiona saw that his eyes were red, and she surmised he had a headache. He'd had a bit to drink at their supper, and she suspected he'd had a bit more after coming aboard.

"Sorry, sir. I...I just needed to get some air." She pushed her sleeves up her arms, then settled her fists on her hips. "But I'm here now, and I'd be pleased if you'd tell me what I am supposed to cook for the crew."

The captain stared at her for a long moment, and she saw confusion register in his face. "I thought you said you could cook," he growled.

"I can, sir. Just tell me what, and I'll get on with it." She glanced around and saw things in a different light this morning. She hadn't noticed last night the dirty disarray in the cooking space. Pots and pans sat unwashed, the stovetop was greasy, and there was grit on the floor, as if it had never been swept. Fiona swallowed her disgust. "And what time meals are to be served," she added, wondering how she was going to prepare anything decent in this filthy mess.

"You can start with oatmeal," he said at last. "It's in the bin over there. We took on fresh water here, so you can cook it in that. And there's biscuits overhead in that cupboard."

"Is there soap to, uh, clean the pots with?" she ventured, gesturing to the stack of dirty cooking pans.

"Clean the pots! What do you think this is, the king's palace?"

Fiona glared back at him, refusing to be intimidated. If he wanted her to cook, he'd have to let her do it her way. "Sir," she said, trying to remain respectful. "My Ma taught me that food, even as plain as ours has always been, tastes better and keeps you from getting sick when it's cooked in clean ware."

Captain Michael just shook his head. "What have I done?" he grumbled, turning to go. "This is your job, not mine," he said gruffly. "Do it. Three meals a day. Starting now."

It was late in the morning, after several crew members had visited the galley grumbling about hunger, when Fiona served up her first dish aboard the *Lady Caroline*. It was indeed oatmeal, cooked in clean water, in a pot she had scrubbed as best she could with some of the same clean water that had recently been taken aboard. Later she would regret using that precious commodity for dishwashing. Water on a sailing ship quickly spoiled and turned slimy in the storage casks and so was prized when still fresh. The oatmeal was savory, because she'd found a stash of salt as she rummaged through her stores, and some not-quite-rancid butter. The men ceased to grumble when they tasted it.

Fiona had never been away from dry land, and she was unprepared for the motion that quickly seized the ship as the anchor was hoisted and the sails filled, sending her off-balance and almost into the still-hot stove. She steadied herself on a rough cabinet and blinked. After a few minutes, the rocking motion turned her stomach, and she feared she was going to be sick.

Quickly, she dashed up the companionway and onto the deck, where the crew was busy setting the sails. She made her way to the front of the vessel and inhaled deeply, trying to settle her queasy stomach.

The weather had turned fair, considering it was Ireland. The sun shone through thin clouds and glinted on the water as they sailed down the river that led to the sea. She watched the walls of Derry growing smaller as they moved away. Beyond those walls, beyond the hills that stretched behind them, was her farm. Her family. Her life up until now. A deep sense of desolation settled around her heart. Alone. She was all alone, even surrounded by the scraggly men of the ship's crew. Her only acquaintance so far, other than the unnamed almost toothless man, was Captain Michael, and she still didn't know what to make of him.

She returned to the galley, and although the motion of the ship continued to unsettle her, she tried to maintain her balance, and as she busied herself, she began to pay it little heed. Her second meal consisted of boiled potatoes and turnips, seasoned with salt and some black meat scraps, cooked up into a stew. She was unsure of how to serve the crew, or when, but around mid-day, Captain Michael appeared in the galley. His mood seemed to have improved, and he instructed one of the crew members to haul the hot cauldron of stew onto the deck where the crew proceeded to help themselves. Fiona had saved back a portion of the stew for herself, but instead she presented it to the captain.

"For you, sir," she said.

He took the dish and spoon and tasted what she'd prepared. After two more spoons full, he handed her back the dish. "Not bad, for a beginner," he remarked. Before she could muster a retort, he continued. "Lucky we were able to take on a few supplies in Londonderry. The crossing took longer than we expected, what with the storm and all. We were close to being out of victuals."

"I...uh, noticed the stores were low," Fiona ventured. "I assume we'll resupply in Liverpool?"

The captain must have taken pity on her at that moment, because his demeanor softened, and he gave her an encouraging smile. "Yes, of course. Thank God that won't be long now. I will ask Mr. Bearden to work with you. He's our ship's quartermaster. Does all the provisioning."

Mr. Bearden turned out to be old snaggly-tooth himself. After serving an evening meal of warm beer, hard biscuits and stewed peas, Fiona was cleaning up the galley as best she could when Mr. Bearden appeared in the doorway. Catching her using the fresh water for cleaning, he swore loudly.

"Bloody hell, girl, you can't use that water for scullery work! It's for the men. They get a ration of it a day before it goes bad."

Fiona turned a full glare on the man. "Do not swear at me, Mr. Bearden. Nobody's told me what I can and cannot do, what I'm supposed to cook, how I'm supposed to do it in a filthy kitchen with wormy flour, and...and..." She broke off, suddenly afraid she might burst into angry tears.

To her surprise, Mr. Bearden let out a hearty, breathy laugh. "High spirited one, ain't ye?" He made his way through the narrow corridor and took a seat on a nearby barrel. "Well, the captain said I's to work with ye until we get to Liverpool, and seein' as how ain't nobody else wants to cook, guess I'd better be nice to ye."

Fiona frowned. "That would be a good start," she replied warily. "That, and helping me learn my job, not just throwing me to the wolves."

Chapter Five

Liverpool was unlike anything she'd ever seen or even could have imagined. Derry had been the outskirts of her life experience, and she'd found it daunting. But Liverpool was something else altogether. Approaching along the Mersey River past a long, broad beach, it seemed to Fiona that the city stretched as far as the eye could see, with steeples and towers, tall buildings and hundreds of houses.

Inside the harbor, she saw other ships, many far larger than the *Lady Caroline*, tied to the dock, with scores of people and a flurry of activity all along the quayside. Wagons seemed to groan beneath the weight of the cargo being offloaded—barrels and crates and large battens of something white—cotton, Mr. Bearden told her. They, too, he said, carried cotton from America to be manufactured into cloth here in England. And sugar and rum from the islands.

Among the crowds she saw strange people, exotic looking, with black skin. The men were clothed only in what looked like swaddling on a baby, and the few women wore dresses that looked as if they were made from rough sacking material. Fiona had never seen a black person before. "Who are those people?" she asked.

"Africans," Bearden told her. "Slaves."

Only then did she see that these people were chained together in small groups, and she suddenly recalled her Da saying that soon young Irish people would meet the same fate. "That's horrible," she murmured.

"'Tis not to my liking either," Bearden said. "But them's worth a lot of money. More lucrative than most cargos." Then he added, almost under his breath, "Thank th' good Lord we ain't in that business."

Until they embarked on their journey to Charlestown, Fiona stayed at an inn run by a respectable-looking matron aptly named Mrs. Stout, whom she helped in the kitchen. "Seeing as how I'm to work for an English family in Charlestown," she told the good dame, "I would like to learn more about English cooking." What she learned to her dismay was that the English liked their food bland. Very bland.

A fortnight later, Mr. Bearden took her back to the ship, escorting her to the captain's quarters. In his cabin, which was spacious and well-lit from the bank of windows that spread across the stern, Captain Michael seemed distraught. "We sail in three days' time," he told her. "I want you and Bearden to make sure we have enough stores for a longer voyage than I expected."

"How much longer?" Fiona asked, alarmed. Truth was, she had no idea how long it took to reach Charlestown, but she'd heard many weeks, maybe months. She had no desire to be cooped up on this ship any longer than she had to be.

"A month, maybe more," he replied. He went to the high windows and gazed out. "I…it's hard to reckon."

"Did you recruit more crew?" she asked. "What about the cook? Did you get another cook?"

The captain turned and shot a funny look at Mr. Bearden. "We'll sail with a full crew this time. And, uh, about the cook. We didn't find one."

"What! But you said…"

"I had planned to, but truth is, the men asked me to keep you on as cook. They're fond of your vittles, as one of them said."

"But…"

"No argument. You agreed when I took you on you'd follow the captain's orders. And they are that you should remain as our cook. Now, about something else," he hurried on, brooking no further conversation about the matter. "The new crew members. You must keep your distance from these men. I promised your father I'd deliver you whole and sound to my client in Charlestown, and I have every intention of doing so, but you must help me by laying low."

Fiona wasn't sure what laying low meant. "You mean stay out of sight?"

"Exactly. Just stay below decks as much as possible and don't invite attention. Some of these men are, well, criminals. They joined the crew to avoid going to jail."

Fiona blinked. "Criminals?"

"Don't be shocked. It's how the system works. The government wants to get rid of them, and they don't want to go to jail, so they sign on as sailors." He hesitated a moment, then added, "Problem is, they don't know a damned thing about sailing. Mr. Bearden and some others of my regular crew will spend precious time training them and getting them into proper shape." He looked directly at Fiona. "That's another reason for you to stay out of sight. There's some things likely to happen you don't want to see."

Fiona's eyes widened, but she said nothing. Resigning herself to her fate, a moment later she asked, "So how many do I cook for now?"

"Thirty-five, at least to start."

Fiona inhaled deeply. "Sir, with all due respect, to get three meals a day for that many people, I'll need a helper in the galley. I can't do that alone."

The captain again glanced at Mr. Bearden. "Can you find her a helper, Bearden? Someone who can be trusted in the galley?"

But Mr. Bearden shook his head. "None's that's with us now, captain. I'll need to go find someone."

The captain nodded. "Go then and make it swift. We sail on Wednesday. You know what to look for."

The night before they were to sail, Mr. Bearden arrived on board and descended the companionway into the galley with a large shipping sack thrown over his shoulder. A large, squirming sack that he set down roughly.

"What's that?" Fiona asked, fearing it was a live animal she might have to butcher.

"'Tis your galley help." With that, Bearden removed the sack and out spilled a filthy, ragged boy, his hands bound with thick rope. He grabbed the boy's arm and pulled him forcibly to his feet. "Stand, boy, and say your name."

The boy's eyes were round and filled with fear when he looked up at Bearden. "Ain't got un," he said in a hoarse whisper.

"Speak up! I said say your name."

The boy's look turned defiant. "I said I ain't got un. Let me go!" He turned and tried to escape up the stairs, but Bearden caught him and thrust him deeper into the galley.

Fiona was horrified as it dawned on her that Bearden must have kidnapped the boy. "Mr. Bearden, please, who is he? Why is he tied up? Where did he come from?"

"Ye ask too many questions, girl. He don't know it yet, but meeting up with me was the best thing to happen to him." With that, he pushed the boy to the floor and lashed his small body to a large, heavy barrel. "There. That'll keep him until we sail." And with that, Bearden returned to the deck, leaving Fiona speechless.

She took a tentative step toward the lad. "Hello," she said quietly.

He glared up at her. "Leeme alone," he growled.

"Are you...uh...thirsty?"

He didn't answer, just stared ahead sullenly.

Fiona was aghast and couldn't think what to do. Obviously, this boy had been taken against his will, but she was in no position to release him. Indeed, she feared him just a bit, he was so wild-looking. She tried to think and recalled the captain's words to Bearden, "Go then. You know what to look for." Was this another common practice in the system, to kidnap young boys and force them into service aboard these ships?

Without asking him again, she brought a cup of water and extended it toward his grubby hands. He looked up at her suspiciously and at first rejected her offer, but she didn't move away. "Here," she said. "Drink it."

At last he took the cup and drank thirstily. Fiona reached into an overhead bin and brought out one of the hard biscuits that were to sustain them on the voyage. Without speaking, she handed it to the boy. He again eyed her with distrust, but in seconds grabbed the food and crammed it into his mouth, eating feverishly. She quickly made him some oatmeal, which he took immediately, nearly swallowing the oats whole.

After a few moments, Fiona tried again. "My name's Fiona," she offered, hoping he would give his at last, but he sat with his head hung forward. She knelt down, but not too close to him. "Can you tell me your name?" His reply was a slight shake of the head. "Do your ma and da know you're here?"

"Ain't got none." The boy's voice was barely audible, but Fiona was getting a picture of this pathetic creature who had been handed into her care. An orphan, a filthy, starving street urchin, now kidnapped and forced into service on the ship. She sighed. Maybe Bearden was right, maybe this was a fortunate turn of fate for him. At least here he wouldn't starve. She didn't untie him, but seeing him nod off, left him to slumber in his new quarters in the galley, thinking this minimal shelter was likely better than the streets of Liverpool.

Before dawn the following morning, she was roused by the sound of men clambering over the deck above her head. She shot out of bed, donned her work dress, and ran to the galley, afraid she was late for serving the crew their breakfast. Only then did she remember the no-name boy who was awake but still tied to the barrel.

"Good morning," she greeted him, hoping she sounded cheerful. He grunted. "Hungry?" she asked and saw his face light up just a bit. He nodded. She had cooked more oatmeal the night before than she'd served him, so she warmed what was left over and gave it to him. "You know you're going with us, don't you?"

He nodded resolutely. "Guess I am at that."

"Do you know you're supposed to help me in the galley here cooking for the crew? That's what they stole you for."

He gave a snort. "Cookin'! What d'I know about cookin'?"

"I suppose not much. So, guess I'll be teaching you then. We've thirty-five hungry sailors to feed three times a day. I'm just one person. I can't do it alone. Are you willing to help me?"

He studied her a minute, she guessed while he considered his options. Seeing none, he replied, "Aye."

"Good then. But it would be helpful if you gave me your name, I mean if we're going to work together."

She saw confusion and shame on his face before he replied, "Was tellin' th' truth. Ain't got no name."

Fiona's heart wrenched. This poor, poor boy. "Well, then, I guess I'll just have to give you one," she said a little too brightly. "How about Daniel?" she asked, not realizing until a few moments later it was her little brother's name, the one who'd died in the pox epidemic. This boy looked nothing like her Daniel, but in some small measure, it made her feel good. "I could call you Danny. Is that all right with you?"

The boy looked at her in wonder and amazement. "You'd…you'd give me a name?"

His obvious gratitude summoned tears, but she blinked them back. "Of course. Everyone needs a name," she managed over a tightness in her throat. "So, will Daniel do?"

The newly-named Daniel actually beamed. "Aye! I'll be Daniel. And I'll work hard for ye, Fiona. Yes, I will. You can bet I will."

"Very well then. I can't untie you, Daniel. Mr. Bearden must be the one to do that, and I'm pretty sure he won't until we're out of sight of land. But I can sort of get us started." Wondering if he'd had a bath in his life, she heated water, handed him a rough bar of lye soap and a rag, and told him to scrub up. They were in the middle of his ablutions when Mr. Bearden thundered down the stairs.

"Good God, girl, what are ye doin'?"

Fiona shot to her feet and eyed Bearden defiantly. "Making him clean enough to prepare your food, sir. Unless you want his filth in your pudding."

Bearden moved to the boy, who cringed away from him. "No worries, boy. We're off now, and there's no goin' back to them streets. Be glad for your escape. If I untie ye, will ye promise to behave and not try any funny business?"

The boy looked past Bearden to Fiona, who indicated he should agree, and so he did.

Bearden released him and had the decency to help him to his feet. "I'm takin' him up for a few minutes. Probably needs to relieve himself," he told Fiona. To the boy, he said, "Don't even think about jumpin' ship, lad. Ye'd never make it to shore, drown for sure."

Fiona recognized the feel of the ship that had now left the dock and put to sea, but this time the rocking didn't make her queasy. She was accustomed to the creaking of the boards and the crack of the sails as they unfurled to the wind. At last, they were on their way to Charlestown!

Chapter Six

As Fiona established a routine that allowed her to prepare the food needed to feed the many hungry sailors, barely finishing one meal before starting the next, Danny proved to be competent help once he learned the ropes. Mr. Bearden kept a close eye on them both and again forbade Fiona to come up on deck.

She grew tired of being confined in such small and close quarters, and one day after she had her work under control, she ventured up the stairs to the deck. The fresh wind that hit her face was delicious! She inhaled deeply and turned her gaze to the sun. It was a breezy day, and above her the full sails blossomed like white moonflowers. Cautiously, she made her way to one side of the ship and looked out across the horizon. From the angle of the sun, she surmised they were on a westerly course. They were on their way to Charlestown! She squinted into the distance, as if searching for her new home.

Suddenly, someone grabbed her roughly by the arm and swung her around, and she found herself facing one of the ugliest men she'd ever seen.

"Well, well, what've we got here?" he leered, grasping her face and turning it toward him. "I believes this be a girlie."

Fiona tried to wrench away from him. "Let me go!" she cried, but the man just laughed.

"Now why would I want to do that, girlie? We's just gettin' to know each other." With that he moved his hand beneath her skirt and began to move it up her leg. "Let's us see if this is indeed a girlie."

Fiona screamed and managed to shake his hand from her leg, but he held her arm firmly and gave a vulgar laugh that came out in a stinking breath. "Ah, feisty one, she is. I likes feisty."

She looked around in panic and saw they had attracted the attention of other sailors who moved closer, watching curiously. She looked up at her captor and said defiantly, "The captain told me that things happen to sailors who get out of line," she snapped. "I believe he said 'unpleasant things.'"

But her attempt at a threat didn't seem to bother the man. "But the captain ain't here, now is he?"

Fiona saw the sailors who'd gathered around move away, and Mr. Bearden appeared. "The captain ain't here, but I am, and you're to let her go, NOW!" With that, he withdrew a long whip from his belt.

The man released Fiona in an instant, but he glared at her. "We ain't finished yet, girlie."

Fiona dashed to the stairs, but before she vanished below, she turned and saw Bearden order several of the men to strip the sailor to his waist and tie him to a mast. Then to her horror, he flogged the man until his back bled. Then he turned to the rest. "Let this be a lesson to ye bastards," he snarled. "Captain warned you to leave the kitchen help alone. She's th' kitchen help, her and th' boy. If ye want to eat on this voyage, and avoid this," he indicated the flogged man who now sagged in his bondage, "ye'll do as the captain ordered. Now, back to work, all of ye."

Just when Fiona thought the worst was over, she saw Bearden and two other men untie her attacker, drag him to the side of the ship, and throw him overboard. She stifled a scream and returned swiftly to the safety of the galley. Only then did she lose her stomach, retching violently into a nearby pan. She was gathering herself together when Bearden appeared in the companionway. His face was red with fury.

"See what ye've done now!" he railed at her. "Gone and caused a lot of trouble. Th' men are 'roused and soundin' mean, but what happened to that bloke will keep 'em in line, for now anyways. The captain told you to stay out of sight. Now you know why."

Fiona couldn't hold back her tears. She felt terrible that her actions had caused a man's torture and death, but she also began to realize that she wasn't free, that this galley was a prison. "I...I didn't mean to cause trouble, Mr. Bearden," she said, regaining control. "I just needed some fresh air. It's tight down here, and I don't know if I'll survive the voyage if I'm trapped down here like a rat in a hole."

"Don't question the captain," he warned.

"Perhaps I need to speak to the captain," she shot back. "Would you let him know that I have been ill? I don't think he wants me to perish on this voyage."

Both of them knew the truth of that. Fiona was of no value as a corpse, very little if she arrived ill or otherwise incapacitated. She didn't know what Captain Michael might fetch for her indenture, but he seemed to think it worth carrying her across an ocean.

Bearden's eyes narrowed. "Stay below, if ye know what's good for ye." And then he was gone.

Danny cowered at the far end of the galley, next to the hatch that led to where their stores lay. Fiona was trembling, but she gave him a reassuring smile. "It's all right," she said, not really believing it. "Do not worry. Come, it's time to work on the midday meal."

That night, after the last meal was served and the galley straightened, Fiona took to her cabin, leaving Danny to sleep on the large sacks of beans and grain in the storage hold. She picked up her fiddle and played a mournful tune which actually made her cry. Her playing was cut off by a sharp rap at her door.

"Who's there?" she asked warily.

"Captain Michael. May I come in?"

She threw back the latch and saw the captain in the dim light. "Yes, sir, of course." She stepped away to give him room to enter the tiny quarters.

"Mr. Bearden has of course reported to me what happened today," he began.

"Yes, sir, I'm sorry, sir," she managed.

"This is why I forbade you to come up on deck, do you understand now?" He reminded her of her father when he was angry with her.

"Yes, sir," she said again. "But, Captain Michael, I don't think I can stand to stay in this hot, stifling place for the months it will take us to reach Charlestown. I will suffocate! I need to walk around, have some fresh air. So does Danny," she added.

She thought she caught a troubled shadow cross his face, but it was so fleeting, she figured she imagined it. He was quiet for a long moment, then he said, "Very well. I understand your needs. Henceforth on this journey, I will have Mr. Bearden escort you on deck for fifteen minutes each day. Will that suffice?"

It wasn't exactly an offer of freedom, but it was also a means to an end, and with Mr. Bearden, they should be safe. "Very well, sir. Thank you," she said.

Captain Michael looked past her at the fiddle and bow that lay on her bunk. "I heard you playing. You're quite good. Could you play a fiddle tune for me now?" He gave her a small smile and added, "Something a little less melancholy?"

Fiona felt a weight lift from her shoulders and happily picked up the instrument. "How about this?" She launched into a favorite that she and her sister had danced to in happier times.

When she finished, the captain applauded lightly. "Very nice. What's the name of that tune?"

"Grey Eagle, sir. It's very traditional."

"Very nice. Perhaps you'd do me the honor of playing for me a little each night, to help this voyage pass more quickly."

Fiona loved music, loved playing the fiddle, and she was grateful for this opportunity. "Yes, sir," she said eagerly, then added, "...if you or Mr. Bearden will escort me to your cabin."

Chapter Seven

They had been at sea a fortnight, and to Fiona's relief, the weather had remained fair with winds that sent the ship swiftly on their westerly course. She and Danny had, as promised, been granted a short time each day on deck, accompanied by Mr. Bearden. She noted that when they walked along the deck, the sailors averted their eyes. She guessed one dead man was enough for them.

In the evenings, Bearden returned and escorted them to the aft of the ship to the captain's quarters. They were spacious and housed a desk, bunk, and comfortable chairs. One night while Fiona was playing a lively tune, Danny slipped two spoons from his pocket and began to beat out a rhythm to accompany the fiddle. Fiona laughed and tossed her head back and nodded, encouraging the boy. Even the captain got in the spirit of the music, tapping his fingers on his desk. At the end, Captain Michael spoke to Mr. Bearden, who had been invited to join the merriment.

"Bearden," he said. "What say you to allowing these two to play for the men?"

Mr. Bearden was obviously not pleased. "I don't think it wise, sir. Remember what happened…"

But the captain cut him off. "I do remember, Mr. Bearden. But in my experience as a captain, I know the importance of maintaining a contented crew. Perhaps Fiona's music will keep them in good spirits. Along with her cooking," he added with a smile.

Fiona didn't much want to do as the captain was suggesting, but she was pleased at his compliments. "I don't know, sir. Would these men set out to harm me?"

The captain eyed Bearden again. "I think not. Half of them are our own men, been with us awhile. They're safe enough, and the others have learned to toe the line. Mr. Bearden, inform those who are off duty to gather on the fo'c'sle after nightfall, and make sure they know punishment will be severe should anyone get out of hand."

"Aye, aye, sir," Bearden said, but left the cabin with a scowl.

Later, as the mid-summer sun sank below the horizon, the captain and Mr. Bearden appeared on deck along with other officers—Mr. Greene, the sailing master, Mr. Bentley, the boatswain, and Mr. Pressley, the ship's carpenter and surgeon—and more than a dozen sailors, those who were off duty or could leave their stations for a short while. "This is Fiona," the captain said, introducing her to the raggedy bunch. "She's been your cook and will be so until the end of the voyage. Do I hear a huzzah for her skills in the galley?"

To her amazement, the men raised their voices and their hands in approval, but it may only have been, she thought quickly, because the captain told them to. Nonetheless, she was encouraged.

He continued, "I've discovered she has more talents as well; she and the boy Danny are musicians." Another huzzah arose spontaneously. "Quiet now. Let's see if I'm mistaken."

At that he nodded to Fiona, who with hands that shook more than a little, placed the fiddle under her chin and played like she'd never played before. Tunes came flying from her fingers, and Danny worked feverishly to keep up with the spoons. Shortly, she heard the sounds of shoes tapping the deck and looked up to see two of the rugged sailors dancing a jig. She glanced nervously at the captain, her eyes inquiring if it was okay to continue, but he was smiling and clapping his hands, so she kept on. In fact, just for fun, she picked up the tempo, challenging the dancers to keep up.

Mr. Bentley, the boatswain, had left the group, and when he returned, he produced an Irish flute and began to play along. He and Fiona played another lively jig together, and a cheer went up at the end of the song. Fiona was flushed and laughing, and for the first time since leaving Ireland, she felt some joy in her heart.

When at last she'd grown tired and had fairly run through her repertoire, she said as much to the captain, who agreed it was time to end the evening. "Back to your stations or your bunks, men," he commanded, "but first, a round of applause for our musicians." A mixture of groans that the evening was ending and applause for Fiona came from the men who rose off the barrels and ship's structures where they'd been sitting. But before they split up, one man started to sing. His voice was deep and resonant, and his song was soon picked up by some of the others. They sang a mournful sailor's tale, telling of the many dangers they faced, including the violent storms at sea.

Fiona listened to the words and the hearty but doleful tune, and gradually the joy of the evening ebbed into the hollow of fear that had been her constant companion on this journey. So far, the weather had held, but she'd heard stories of the storms that sent these ships and all those aboard to the bottom of the ocean. Fiona looked up into the now star-filled sky. It was nearly summer solstice, she reckoned, and late in the night. Half a year since her winter solstice birthday. She wished she'd kept a record of each day in that book Granny had given her, which until this moment she'd almost forgotten. She would ask the captain for the date on the morrow and keep better records.

That night in her dreams, Fiona saw Granny walking up the steep hill toward her small house. She tried to call out, to catch up with the old woman, but no matter how hard she tried, Granny was always far in the distance. At last, for a moment, her beloved grandmother turned, looked directly at her, and smiled. Something passed between them at that moment, a spark, a knowing, and then she was gone.

Fiona awoke with a start and a terrible presentiment that Granny had just died. Sliding her hand beneath her pillow, she brought out the smooth stone with the ancient carvings, and she knew it was true; she could feel it. Her Granny had passed over. But oddly, instead of grief, Fiona experienced a sense of protection and well-being, as if Granny's spirit was with her now, and always would be. She ought to cry, she thought, but couldn't. She'd cried enough on this journey. No, in her heart, she heard Granny encouraging her, telling her to be strong, no matter what.

Fiona clenched the stone so tightly it hurt her fingers, but she used it to focus her mind. She brought a vivid image of her Granny to her inner vision and almost felt the old woman's spirit enter her own body. Fiona straightened. Her fear subsided and renewed strength and determination filled her soul.

* * *

A few days later, during her brief exercise on deck with Mr. Bearden and Danny, Fiona realized the ship had changed direction and was now headed on a more southerly course. "Is this the way to Charlestown?" she asked Bearden one afternoon.

He didn't answer right away, and his silence troubled her. "In a roundabout way, I suppose," he replied at last.

"What do you mean, roundabout? We're sailing south now, am I right? Shouldn't we continue to go to the west?"

"Ye ask too many questions," Bearden growled. "These're answers you'll have to get from the captain." With that, he escorted them back to their quarters belowdecks and the work of preparing the evening meal.

When she and Danny raised the food up the companionway to Bearden on deck that evening, she called to him, "Mr. Bearden, would you kindly ask Captain Michael if I may speak with him this evening?"

She didn't hear his reply, but later that night, after the meal was finished and the galley cleaned, Captain Michael appeared in the companionway. "I heard you wish a word with me," he said.

Fiona wiped her hands on a cloth and looked at him. He wasn't a handsome man, but had a fair chin that was clean-shaven, unlike the rest of the crew. He wore his uniform this evening, although she'd seen him dressed more casually at times on this trip. Maybe he considered this a formal call.

"Aye, I did, sir. I have a question concerning our route." She saw him chuckle.

"Now in addition to being our cook and musician, you'll also be the captain?"

"Ah, nay sir, but I sense we're not on the same course as when we left. Are we not still headed to Charlestown?"

The captain took a seat on one of the narrow steps. "Well, yes we are. But when I was in Liverpool, I received new orders from the ship's owner, the man I sail for." He paused and seemed reluctant to go on, but Fiona held her tongue and waited, curious as to what the change in plans might be, and by how many weeks it would extend the voyage.

"He's asked me to carry a different kind of cargo on this trip," he said at last, sighing and running his fingers through his thinning hair. "Cargo we're on our way to fetch."

"What kind of cargo?" She hadn't witnessed the ship being loaded for the journey, so she had no idea of what kind of cargo they held.

Captain Michael eyed her evenly. "Slaves."

Chapter Eight

The equatorial heat was suffocating as they sailed along the west coast of Africa. Fiona had never endured hot, humid weather, and her work in the galley became almost insufferable. She managed to acquire two head scarves from Mr. Bearden's quartermaster stores, and she and Danny wore them tied around their foreheads, much like the crew members on deck, to absorb the sweat before it fell into their eyes.

When at last they dropped anchor, the ship suddenly seemed eerily quiet after the motion and noise of the ocean voyage, as if it had been deserted. Then Fiona heard shouts and two loud splashes, followed in a short time by the sounds of creaking wood and winding windlass, and she felt the ship shudder from time to time. Curious, she crept to the top of the companionway to see the crew off-loading large crates and barrels into longboats. Mr. Bearden had told her they were taking guns and barrels of rum or brandy to the slave traders in exchange for the humans who'd been captured by rival tribes and sold into slavery.

Shortly, Captain Michael went aboard one of the longboats, and Mr. Bearden boarded the other. Fourteen crew members were in each boat, rowing two abreast. Few were left on board: the sail master, Albert Greene, who was in charge in the captain's absence, Mr. Bentley, the boatswain who had become her musical partner in their nearly nightly gatherings on deck, and three sailors. Summoning her courage and warning Danny not to wander too far from the galley, she gathered her skirts and made her way to the aft deck, where Mr. Greene stood watching the progress of the longboats through a telescope.

"Beg pardon, sir. May I ask you a question?" she asked.

Greene turned and glared at her. "I thought you weren't supposed to leave the galley."

"Most of the men are gone, and there's some things I need to know about what's happening, since I'm to cook for more people now."

He remained silent, his back to her, but she persevered. "Where will we put these people?" she asked. "Will they stay on deck? How many will there be? And how am I supposed to feed them?"

"That's more than one question."

Fiona gritted her teeth. "I'll rephrase my request. May I ask you several questions?"

"You already have." His words were terse, and his attitude infuriated her, but she remained silent, waiting. At last he replied, "They'll go in the 'tween decks. Between the main deck and the hold." He turned, frowned at her and huffed. "You're annoying me. Leave!"

Annoyed herself, she gave up and sought out Mr. Bentley, to ask one critical question: "How many will there be for me to feed?"

"Might be as many as fifty. We're to take on as many as we can hold. They say some will die on the crossing. The more we carry, the more might survive for sale over there."

Fiona was aghast. "Fifty! Mr. Bentley, how am I going to feed fifty more people?"

"Not three times a day. That's for the ship's crew only. No, these will get something once or twice a day, probably mush or horse beans. Something you can make a goodly quantity of all at once."

Fifty people! Stashed in the dark in the dank recesses of the ship. No wonder some would die. And they were her's to feed. Dear God in heaven! What was she going to do?

Chapter Nine

Over the next two days, boats ferried small groups of Africans to the *Lady Caroline*. There, Samuel Pressley, the ship's carpenter who also served as something of a doctor, examined them, and any who were apparently ill were returned to shore. "Let them be somebody else's problem," he told the captain. "It'll be hard enough to keep the healthy ones alive."

Fiona and Danny watched wide-eyed at the procession of frightened, dirty people who came on board, linked together with heavy chains, clad in nothing except loincloths. Even the women were bare breasted. The children were mostly naked. There was a girl who appeared to be about her own age or just a little younger, and one heavily pregnant woman. All were weeping and wailing, a sound Fiona would remember all her life.

Mr. Bearden had re-provisioned the galley as best he could, bringing on board food Fiona had never heard of, much less knew how to cook. Yams. Horse beans. Palm oil. "Boil 'em and mash 'em up," Bearden instructed how to prepare this primitive fare. "I was told they like that pasty stuff. I tried some onshore." He made a face. "Tastes like dung to me."

At last the "cargo" was loaded, the ship provisioned, and sails set, heading northwest, to Charlestown at last. But two days into the voyage, it became clear to Fiona that she and Danny, even with Mr. Bearden's occasional help, could not keep up with the challenge of feeding both the crew and the slaves. She had tried with all her strength to keep pots of water boiling, vegetables peeled and cooking, and creating vittles fit to eat. The horse beans disgusted her, and the yams eluded her. With only a bulkhead between the galley and the imprisoned slaves, their cries and wails assailed her, and she found herself near tears when Captain Michael appeared in the galley.

"How goes it, Fiona?" he asked, taking a long look around the galley.

She considered lying, but then thought better of it. What was the point in telling him that everything was fine when it wasn't? She looked him square in the eye, feeling her latent anger begin to surface. "It isn't going well at all, captain. It's too much for the two of us." The anger boiled over, and she clenched her fists and let it out. "At first, I was to feed nineteen, only as far as Liverpool. Then that became thirty-five and no new cook. Now it's thirty-five plus the forty or more," she said, indicating the direction of the hold. The took a deep breath and tried to calm down. "Sir, with all due respect, I need more help."

The captain frowned. "I didn't take you for a whiner."

"Whiner! I'm not whining! You asked. I told you how it is. You and the crew seem to be a bit spoiled to my cooking, I daresay, and if you want me to keep it up, send me somebody else to help do some of this heavy cooking."

"Fiona, I cannot spare one single sailor. If we are going to make safe harbor in Charlestown before the end of fall, I need all hands doing the work of the ship."

Even if they have to go hungry? she wanted to snap at him, but she held her tongue. Then an idea occurred to her. "Sir, seems to me we have many on board doing nothing but that awful crying and chanting over there. Suppose any of them might be released to me to become kitchen help?"

Captain Michael looked at her as if she'd lost her mind. "That is out of the question! Let one of them loose, he'd likely start a riot, or try to jump overboard. They're big, strong men, Fiona. Didn't you see? You wouldn't be safe with any of them, even if they were willing to help."

"I wasn't thinking of the men," she replied. "I saw a girl when they were coming aboard. About my age, I think. Maybe younger, but she looked strong and healthy. Maybe her, or one of the other women."

The captain considered that a moment, but before he could answer, another idea occurred to Fiona. "Besides, I don't know how to prepare all those yams you brought aboard, which I suppose is their regular food. I can't get the yams to taste good at all unless I fry them up, and with the ship underway and all the motion, that isn't going to work. I won't risk getting burnt by that hot oil. Maybe one of the Africans could show me how to cook them."

He glared at her. "You're a troublemaker, Fiona. I won't have it."

"Then toss me overboard like you did that other troublemaker," she shot back. "I never signed on to cook for anybody," she shouted at him. "I've done as I have been asked. I'm not a troublemaker. I...I..." At this moment, her reserve of strength broke down and vanished. She crumpled onto a sack of rice and dropped her head. "I'm not going to make it through this voyage like this, Captain Michael. I can't sleep at night with all that racket from the slave quarters, and by day, I'm trying but I can't keep up with cooking for this many people. Danny's a good helper, but he's just a lad. Isn't even very strong."

The captain didn't reply, and when she looked up, she saw him leaving up the companionway. So much for that, she thought angrily. What difference did it make to the captain that she needed more hands in the galley? After all, his sailors were likely pushed to their limits as well, she supposed. And as for slaves, well, she and Danny might as well be that. Galley slaves. And there wasn't a thing she could do about it. Jumping overboard didn't seem an appealing option.

Chapter Ten

After the captain left, Fiona took a sip of water and tried to calm down. Her mind was racing, trying to figure a way to make their enormous workload more efficient. She and Danny were chopping some smoked meat and cooked the turnips that would be dinner for the crew, and deep into her thoughts, she didn't hear Mr. Bearden shuffle down the steps into the galley.

"So, I hear ye've gone and done rattled the captain's cage again," he growled.

Fiona jumped and turned to face him, instantly alarmed. Had he come to get rid of another troublemaker? "Sorry. I don't know what you are speaking of," she lied.

Bearden went to the stovetop and peered into the large kettle in which the turnips and some potatoes were stewing. "Oh, yes, you know exactly what I'm speaking of," he said. "I'm to be in charge of finding you yet more help in the galley." He looked her up and down. "I'd'a thought you'd be up to it what with Danny and all, but no, you have to whimper and ask for more."

For the second time that afternoon, Fiona lost her temper. "I am not whimpering, Mr. Bearden, so just stop it. I told the captain what I need to keep your crew fed and those poor souls alive. I'm doing my best, and when I give out, maybe they'll make you do the cooking."

Her face was burning, and she was trembling, not sure what would come next. But she was sure of one thing, she wasn't going to take this from Mr. Bearden or the captain. Then, to her utter astonishment, Bearden broke out in a hearty laugh.

"I told the captain you'd be trouble," he said between guffaws. "Guess he's found that out on his own or he wouldn'a asked me to do what I came down here to do."

Fiona eyed him warily. "Which is...?"

Bearden turned to Danny. "Watch those pots, boy. I have to take her somewhere. We'll be back when our business is done."

With that, he took Fiona by one arm and turned her toward the companionway. "Up you go," he said and waited while she clambered up the narrow steps. On deck, he led her toward the aft of the ship, stopping abruptly at a hatch that covered the hold. Then he turned to her and frowned. "The captain said this was your idea."

"What?"

"He said you thought there might be one of 'em could help you, although how you think that is more'n I can figure."

Fiona was astonished. The captain had actually heard her! But after blurting her idea of using one of the African women to help her, she'd not thought how that would work. Or wouldn't.

Mr. Bearden called for several sailors to gather round the hatch, then he raised the grated cover and laid it back across the deck. Fiona saw there was a similar set of steps as in the galley companionway leading down into the darkness. Confused, she looked at Bearden, who pointed into the dark hole. "We're going to get that help you say you so desperately need." He descended the narrow stairs, then reached up to take her hand. "Come on, then. You're wasting time."

To her horror, Fiona finally grasped what she was expected to do. She was to go down into that terrible place, the place of darkness and despair, of the wailing and crying, to find one of them for her kitchen help. She held onto the side rails tightly as she went, wanting to close her eyes but not daring to. Suddenly a horrible stench met her nose, and she gagged. When she reached the 'tween deck floor, Bearden steadied her and waited for her eyes to adjust to the dim light. He signaled for another sailor to come along too, a well-armed sailor, she noted.

"Watch where you step," Bearden warned. "There's shit all over."

Fiona had never seen anything like the sight that met her eyes. All those black people, barely visible in the midnight darkness, chained to the sides of the ship, and to one another. Only the whites of their eyes were truly visible, peering through the darkness, staring at them. Staring at her. They were quiet now. No moaning, no wailing, no chanting. Fiona shuddered, wishing this was a bad dream.

"So, where is she?" Mr. Bearden asked.

"Who?"

"The girl you told the captain about."

Fiona frantically thought back to her conversation with the captain and remembered she had mentioned a girl she'd seen coming aboard. But how could she remember exactly what she looked like? How could she even see her in this dungeon?

The other sailor, who had apparently been down here before, indicated for them to follow him along the narrow center aisle that separated two groups of people. Fiona realized that the women were on one side, the men on the other. The sailor pointed at one of the women.

"That her, Mr. Bearden?" he asked.

Fiona followed his finger and saw he was pointing at a nearly naked young woman, a girl really. She forced herself to look into the girl's eyes, but couldn't hold her gaze there long.

Quickly, she looked across the rows of upturned faces of the other women held in chains. They all appeared older, except for one very small child. She looked back at the girl, whose expression registered something between insolence and fear.

"Yes," Fiona uttered. "I believe that is the one. But, I...I don't know, Mr. Bearden, what, how...?" she stammered.

"Ye should'a thought of that before, missy," he groused. "'Tis too late now." He turned to the sailor. "Bring her forward. Let's get a better look."

The sailor reached across one row of women and took the girl's arm, propelling her toward the aisle. Her chains rattled and hit two of the women on the front row as she was dragged past them. Mr. Bearden took her arm and turned her toward Fiona.

"Look again. If this is the one, we'll bring her up for ye. From there, she'll be your charge, but she's not t' be let out of the galley, or your sight." He paused, then added, "There'll be hell t' pay if she gets away," he warned.

Fear ripped through Fiona. This girl was, in essence, going to be her slave! The thought was repulsive but then another notion occurred to her. By taking her on in the galley, she would be rescuing her from this sewer where the other poor wretches languished. "Yes, sir, I understand, Mr. Bearden. But, if you remember, I run a clean galley. I will need her to be washed."

Fiona was helped back up the steps and onto the deck, where she saw Captain Michael standing on the aft deck, observing the action, his face grim. Next came the sailor who had cut the girl's chain. He'd released her from the others but had left the chain in place in the shackle around her ankles. The girl struggled up the stairs, then was dragged bodily out onto the deck by the rough sailor. Mr. Bearden followed, then shut and latched the hatch. He turned to the captain.

"'Tis done, sir. What shall we do with her now? Miss Fiona says she must be washed before she'll allow her in the galley." His tone openly taunted Fiona.

Fiona now saw wild fear in the girl's eyes, and she felt a deep sorrow for her. She reflected that the girl wasn't that much different from how Danny had been when he was brought into her care. Dirty. Against her will. Frightened and confused.

"I'll take her," she said firmly, looking up at the captain. "Yes, she needs to be washed, but not in the sight of thirty-five sailors. It's only decent that I as a woman do that."

The captain looked amused. "Suit yourself. Just make sure she's secure. I understand the young ones bring a good price at the market."

At that moment, Fiona hated Captain Michael. Hated Bearden and all the others. Hated what she was participating in. Good God, she was in the slavery business herself now. Still, she nodded to Bearden. "Can you bring her along to the galley? I'll take over from there."

She heard Bearden chuckle, murmuring something to the effect that she should be careful what she asked for.

Chapter Eleven

The galley was steaming hot in the tropical summer day, but the girl shook uncontrollably. She was naked except for a cloth tied around her waist that barely covered her lower body. She was young, breasts still undeveloped but starting to bud. Her eyes cut from Fiona to Danny and back, fearful of what was about to happen to her.

Fiona ordered Danny not to stare and sent him to fetch some clean sea water. When he'd left the galley, she turned to look at the girl fully for the first time. "Don't be afraid," she said softly, although she knew the girl wouldn't understand her language. Fiona reached out her hand and said, "Friend."

Reluctantly the terrified girl touched Fiona's fingertips, then pulled away. Fiona pointed to herself and said, "Fiona. My name's Fiona." Pointing to the girl, she asked "Name?""

After a few tries, a glimmer of understanding lit the girl's eye, and she shyly pointed at Fiona and said in a low voice, "Viona."

Fiona pointed again to the girl, and without asking verbally, indicated with her hands for her to speak her own name. Back and forth this went for a few moments, when suddenly the girl got the idea. "Aalisyah."

"Alisa?"

The girl gave her a small smile, then corrected her. "Aalisyah," and Fiona heard the difference. "Alicia."

Danny returned with the water, which they put on the stove to warm. Fiona introduced Danny to Alicia, who quickly grasped his name, calling him Tanny. By the time the water was hot enough for her bath, they had three words among them: Viona, Alicia, and Tanny.

***

The days at sea became tedious and boring, despite the heavy workload. Alicia proved to be a fast learner, and indeed she taught Fiona how to cook the yams and mash them with a stick, the way her people liked them. The three managed to settle into a work routine, and Fiona even convinced Captain Michael to allow the girl to walk with them on deck for their brief respite from the heat of the galley. Fiona was grateful as she watched Alicia turn her face to the wind and take in a deep breath. Air was life as much as the food they prepared or the water they drank.

One night after Danny and Alicia were bedded down on the supply bags in the galley, Fiona went into her tiny cabin and shut and latched the door. She was grateful that the captain had allowed Alicia to help her with the cooking, and had even agreed, albeit not without a fight, to her joining their brief deck stroll each day. Fiona had made an uneasy peace with her own fate, but something was troubling her that she couldn't quite name. She took out her father's fiddle and began strumming the strings mindlessly. Plucking them, not caressing with the bow. She thought about the vast, seemingly endless ocean she viewed from on deck. There was no way out, no way off this ship. It was as if they were stranded on a little floating island. They had been at sea less than a week. How many more to go before they were on solid ground again?

She picked up the bow and began playing a mournful tune, which only served to send her spirits even lower. Shortly, a light knock came at her door.

"Who's there?" Had Captain Michael returned?

A small voice answered. "Aalisyah."

Fiona opened the door a crack and peered into the face of the young girl. She didn't appear to be distressed or crying. Instead, she had a soft smile on her face. Fiona indicated for her to come into the cramped cubicle, whereupon the girl spied the fiddle. She reached out for it, and Fiona started to slap her hand away, but something in the girl's look stopped her. She would see what would happen next. If she did anything to break her Da's fiddle, the captain could have her back for sure.

But Alicia picked up the fiddle and held it sideways. She plucked at the strings, but instead of producing the mindless sounds Fiona had made, her fingers passed nimbly over the fret and strings, creating a lively tune, although the sound was totally foreign to Fiona.

When she had finished, she shyly handed the fiddle back to Fiona, who took it in hand and turned it to play as Alicia had, but her efforts came to naught. She gave it over to the girl again and said, "Play another?"

There seemed no need at the moment for words. The instrument served as an interpreter.

Alicia played it her way, then Fiona picked up the bow and played a fiddle tune. As they finished, the two young women looked at one another, and Fiona saw both intelligence and beauty in Alicia's unlined black face. She fought back tears to consider what her fate might be. Instead, she pointed to the instrument. "Fiddle," she said.

But Alicia laughed and shook her head. She took the fiddle, held it her way, strummed it vigorously and said, "*ngoni.*"

52

Chapter Twelve

Fiona had begun to keep a daily record in her granny's book, noting her activities and what foods she had prepared. There'd been an episode of the flux among the Africans, and only with her insistence that they be cleaned up and given proper water did they manage to keep all but two alive and in relatively good health.

She figured it was late August the day Captain Michael summoned Fiona to his quarters and gave a warning. "We're nearing the Caribbean, but I fear we're in for bad weather ahead," he informed her, although how he knew that bad weather was coming was beyond her ken. She'd seen a cloudless sky when she came from the galley to his cabin. "The barometer's dropping swiftly," he explained. "This is a bad time of year to be caught in this part of the ocean. It's often a season of terrible storms. The hurricanes."

His worried expression sent a chill through Fiona. "What does that mean for us, sir?"

"It means everything must be lashed down, and I do mean everything. Douse the fires in the galley. Lash every bit of equipment to something stable, something built as part of the ship if possible. Keep Danny and Alicia down there with you, and if the storm hits, lash them and yourself to the ship. You cannot see the storm just yet, but the barometer doesn't lie. It is out there. Maybe within twelve hours or so. Mr. Greene will do his utmost to avoid it, but it's difficult to know which way to sail. In the meantime, I want all precautions taken. Do I make myself clear?"

Fiona swallowed hard and nodded. "Yes, sir," she uttered, then added, "What about the slaves? Don't we need to secure them as well?"

The captain looked grim. "For once, their chains will come in handy. They'll remain in the 'tween decks. They'll be knocked about a bit, but they should be secure enough. Just hope we don't take on water."

Over the next few hours, she and Danny, with help from Alicia when she understood her instructions, shut the galley down. There would be no food served from here for a while, even if they avoided the storm. It would take time to fire up the stoves again, and even longer to prepare meals. In the meantime, she took a large basket of the hard biscuits up to the deck and handed them out to the sailors. "Captain says it may be a terrible storm, and I won't be feeding you for some time. Eat this now while you can."

The activity on deck was frantic. She could see spars and rigging being dismantled and tied down on deck. Sails were being furled to the yards, leaving bare poles except for the minimum sails needed to make headway. Now she saw threatening bluish clouds in the sky to the east, as if the storm had followed them from Africa. They seemed to grow as she stood there watching for a moment. Glancing toward the aft deck, she could see Mr. Greene at the helm, accompanied by Captain Michael. They both looked worried and troubled. The rest of the officers were nowhere in sight, except Mr. Bearden, who came running toward her like a mad man.

"Get in your galley, girl!" he shouted. "Go! Get out of the way!"

As soon as she was down the companionway steps, Fiona heard the heavy thud of the hatch cover closing her in and the slide of the latch securing it firmly shut. A single lantern remained lit, barely illuminating the darkness of the small galley. She shuddered with unadulterated fear.

Looking at her two fellow inmates in this now suffocating prison, she saw they too were terrified. She knew she couldn't let them see her own fear, and so she said with forced brightness, "Well, we can't cook now, so we might as well have some music."

She fetched the fiddle from her cabin, but before returning to the galley, she took the talisman from her satchel and traced the intricate circles on its smooth stone surface. "Dear God in heaven, protect us all from harm," she prayed silently, then slipped the stone into the pocket of her dress and brought the fiddle into the galley.

For the next several hours, the three huddled below decks, sometimes playing music and singing, but as the sounds of the storm grew louder, Fiona put away the fiddle. Using some heavy rope, she tied Danny to one side of a heavy post in the middle of the galley, then secured Alicia to the other side, all the while trying to soothe the frightened girl. "It will be all right," she said calmly, not really believing it. She doused and secured the lantern, then managed to lash herself to another smaller post near her cabin door.

Outside the wind howled, and the ship shuddered under the onslaught of the waves. She felt it rise and fall steeply as the troughs of water deepened. The noise in the galley was deafening, increased by the banging of the pans against the barrels and crates and walls of the adjacent storage hold. Alicia was screaming, and Danny cried. Fiona braced herself for what she feared was the inevitable, wondering what it was going to be like to die.

For hours, the ship was tossed about mercilessly. At one point, she heard the sound of splintering wood and a loud crash as one of the masts broke and fell to the deck. Water began to seep in through the hatch, and it dripped directly onto Fiona's face. She could taste the salt as the sea water ran down her cheek. She tried to wipe it away, but more kept coming. She didn't dare untie herself to find a cloth to seal the leak, and soon they were ankle deep in water on the floor of the galley.

The air was tight, hot, and wet, and Fiona found it hard to breathe, harder still to stay awake. She slouched forward against her bonds, fighting sleep but succumbing for brief moments. The others had grown quiet. She couldn't see them in the dark, and she called out to them. Danny grunted a response, and she heard a whimper from Alicia, so she knew they were still alive.

In one lucid moment, she had another terrifying thought: what if when the storm passed, no one was alive but the three in the galley? How would they get out if no one was left to open the hatch? Clinging desperately to consciousness, her imagination began to run away with her, galloping into the darkest corners of her fears. She tried to take in a breath to keep from crying out, but she choked on the stale air. Then from somewhere she heard her Granny call her name. "Fiona!"

"Granny!" Fiona called aloud, but it wasn't her Granny; it was only her imagination, reaching for comfort from a woman she'd never see again. Not on this side of heaven, at least. And then she thought, maybe I am on the edge of heaven. Maybe Granny can see what's happening, and she's waiting for me to come to her. Maybe I'm about to cross over...

That was her last conscious thought as she sagged weakly against the rope that bound her and blacked out.

Chapter Thirteen

She awoke to rough hands shaking her and releasing her from the bonds, and she fell like a dead weight into the arms of Mr. Bearden. She inhaled fresh salty air coming from somewhere above her, and she drew it in greedily, gradually clearing the fog that was in her brain. Looking up, she saw that his face was bloody and bruised. "Dear God, what happened to you?" she asked him, gathering herself abruptly and standing on her own two feet.

"Storm," was all he said, but his eyes belied a deep grief, and Fiona knew it must have been terrible for those on deck. "Mr. Pressley needs you," he told her. He untied Danny and Alicia and instructed them not to come up on deck. "You two, make order out of this mess," he barked, indicating the inches of water on the floor and the things that had come loose and were now floating over the rough boards.

"Yes, sir," Danny replied in a small, shaky voice.

On deck, utter chaos reigned. The ship had weathered the storm, but it was seriously damaged and had taken on water, not from a shattered hull, but rather from the enormous waves that had pounded it for hours. Men dashed about, trying to sort out the damage to the ship, raise sail in still brisk winds, and help the many injured attend their wounds.

Mr. Bearden led her below to the captain's quarters, where Mr. Pressley attended a badly wounded sailor. Pressley didn't look up but acknowledged her presence with a harsh, "Get over here and hurry!" She rushed to his side, and under his direction, held a gaping wound shut with her bare hands while he stitched the man's belly together with twine normally used for sail repair.

Over the next few hours, she and Mr. Pressley did the best they could for the many who had sustained injuries during the storm. Most were broken bones, cuts and bruises. She learned that several had been washed overboard. "What about the slaves?" she inquired, suddenly remembering them. "Have any survived?"

Captain Michael and Mr. Greene had been nearby, studying charts laid out on his large desk. They both looked up abruptly at her question, as if in the confusion of the aftermath of the storm, they'd forgotten their cargo was human. The captain called out, "Mr. Bearden! Take some men and go below." He returned to the map, muttering something about hoping there was something left to sell when they arrived.

Fiona was helping set a broken arm when Bearden returned to report that the slaves appeared to be mostly intact. "Looks like one man's ankle snapped where it was shackled to the hold. Others likely have broken bones. And that woman's about to have her baby."

Fiona's head jerked up. "What! I must go to her!"

Mr. Pressley growled. "Leave her be. I need you here."

She stared at him. "How can you say that? Seems like we're almost done with most of the worst injuries. She'll die down there, and so will the child."

"So be it. I don't give a damn about them. My job is to attend the crew."

Fiona looked frantically at Captain Michael. "And you, captain, do you care so little for the lives of those you've stolen from their homes to sell like cattle in a market?" She was furious.

"That will be all, Fiona," he replied harshly. "Mr. Pressley needs you here."

She thought furiously for a way to change his mind. Then, "if one of them has shattered his ankle, he'll be of little value at that market, sir. If the woman dies, she'll be of no value whatsoever. If we save the woman and the child lives, that will give you another warm body to replace one of those who has died on this voyage."

Captain Michael rolled his eyes, then looked at Bearden. Bearden shrugged and gave him a rueful grin. "Hate to say it, cap'n, but she's right again. It's all about the money, don't you know."

The captain turned his back to them and stared out of the high bank of windows for a long moment, then turned, and without looking at him, spoke to Mr. Pressley. "Is she correct that you've attended to the most seriously wounded, Mr. Pressley?"

"Yes, sir, but..."

"Then I release her from duty helping you. Mr. Bearden, take her, and..." he broke off, and Fiona could tell he was working hard to control his temper. He took in a deep breath, then finished, "let her help the wench as best she can. I don't want her in my sight again for a long while."

* * *

The noise of the weeping and wailing in the 'tween decks met her ears before she lowered herself into the abyss. She felt warm water swishing over her feet as she made her way in the dim light toward the side of the ship where the women were chained. They grew silent when they saw her and moved away to make room for her to find the pregnant woman. It wasn't difficult; she lay on her back, moaning in pain.

"Help me," Fiona called to the men who had accompanied her. "Help me. We must move her out of here."

"Now wait a minute," Mr. Bearden shouted. "The captain didn't allow that."

"He allowed that I was to help her as best I can, Mr. Bearden. I cannot help her at all here. We must take her out of this filth or the child is likely to drown in it as it's born."

"And take her where?" Bearden wanted to know. "The captain's bunk?"

His sarcasm never ceased to amaze, and amuse, Fiona, even in this dire circumstance. "I don't think the captain wishes to see me at the moment," she replied with equal sarcasm. "Take her to my bunk instead."

With great difficulty, two burly sailors unchained the woman and hauled her, writhing and crying, up the stairway, across the deck, and down the stairs into the galley. Alicia cried out in joy when she saw the woman and ran to her, and Fiona understood there was a close bond between the two. Later she learned this was Alicia's mother.

Alicia pressed her hand against the woman's swollen belly. "*Abofra?*" Her mother calmed somewhat at seeing her daughter. She nodded, and then another contraction took her breath away.

Fiona had sewn a new nightdress from the fabric Granny had given her, and she laid it across her own narrow bunk, instructing the sailors to place the woman upon it. "Now leave," she ordered, and the sailors, obviously relieved, made a dash for the companionway.

Frightened and exhausted, Fiona fought to remain composed in the midst of this new kind of storm. She had helped Granny deliver a baby, but only once. Could she do this by herself? She ordered Danny to fire up the wood stove as quickly as he could, and to boil up all the cleaning rags he could find. She indicated to Alicia to stand by her mother's side and hold her hand, but to her surprise, the girl pushed her aside and took over as midwife. *"Me boa awoo,"* she said.

Before she could argue, Alicia was inside the tiny cabin, pressing on her mother's belly and speaking to her in their native language. It was a soothing sound, and Fiona saw that Alicia was not afraid and knew what to do. And that her mother was now settled down and working at giving birth in a way that was natural for both of them.

The baby, a boy, was born safely shortly thereafter.

***

Since the storm and the baby's birth, Fiona had spent her time below repairing the galley and resuming her duties as cook and had not wanted to go on deck and meet up with the captain or Mr. Bearden. She'd kept Alicia's mother and the newborn in her bunk, never thinking of returning them to the slave quarters. She'd been unable to determine a name for the mother and had considered giving her one, as she had done with Danny, but then decided against it. She did not want to get too close to these people, to feel too deeply for them, because it would hurt too much when they were sold into bondage.

The storm had blown the ship off-course, and in a scant three days, despite having lost one mast, the *Lady Caroline* limped into a small bay near an island in water so blue it nearly hurt Fiona's eyes to look into its jewel-like depths. As soon as the sails were furled and the anchor was set, the crew unlashed the two longboats and splashed them into the water. Fiona left the galley and watched from the rail as a dozen or more sailors clambered down into the longboats. Several wore their arms in slings, others were heavily bandaged. All were eager to get off the ship and onto dry land. She would like that very much herself but wasn't eager to confront the captain on one more issue. She was mesmerized by the amazingly blue water and was unaware when Mr. Bearden came to her side.

"Is all well with…uh, the baby thing?" he asked awkwardly.

Fiona turned to him with a smile. "It is, Mr. Bearden, thanks to you and those other men. You saved two lives."

Bearden rubbed his face, and Fiona saw the weariness, and sadness, in his faded blue eyes. "I've somethin' for ye," he said, reaching into his coat pocket. He drew out Mr. Bentley's wooden flute and handed it to Fiona. "I think he'd want you to have it."

"Mr. Bentley? Why would he want that?" she replied, not comprehending.

"Mr. Bentley was lost in the storm, Fiona. Went overboard trying to save a mate."

Fiona closed her eyes against the glare of the midday Caribbean sun. "No," she whispered. Then a moan made its way from her heart to her lips, a fierce, unquenchable cry of despair, born of exhaustion, fear, and sorrow. "No!" She crumpled to the deck and began to sob uncontrollably. She wept for Mr. Bentley. She wept for the sailors lost and injured in the storm.

She wept for the slaves, for the new baby, for Alicia. She wept for herself as well. She wondered briefly and not a little bitterly how her father had ever thought this would be a better life for her.

And then her thoughts ceased altogether as she lost consciousness.

CHAPTER FOURTEEN

Fiona awoke in a strange bunk, then sat up abruptly, realizing she was in the captain's cabin. "Good morning, Fiona," a voice greeted her, and she saw Captain Michael sitting serenely behind his desk, watching her with an amused grin on his lips.

"What? Where...?"

"You passed out on the deck yesterday afternoon. Bearden didn't know quite what to do with you, with that woman still in your bunk and all, so he brought you here."

Fiona had no idea how long she had slept, but it obviously had been many hours, and new energy surged through her. She slid her feet to the floor and straightened her dress, which was soiled with blood and muck. "I'm very sorry, Captain. I didn't mean to..."

The captain cut her off. "Don't be sorry, Fiona. You have done a commendable job on this journey. A very difficult job on a very difficult voyage. It is I who must apologize. I who have perhaps asked more of you than I should have."

Suddenly her Granny's words echoed in her mind: *You must be brave...you will be needed.* She *had* been needed on this journey, and she was gratified at the captain's praise.

He told her what had transpired while she slept. The ship had arrived at an island called St. Croix, owned by the Danes. Here they re-provisioned and replenished the fresh water supply. "This is one of the sugar islands," he explained. "Major plantations here raise sugar cane, and they're offering to buy all of our slaves. I'll have some explaining to do to the ship owner's clients who are expecting them in Charlestown. But," he paused, "I can get a good price for them and be done with the loathsome transaction. The profit is all the ship's owner really cares about anyway."

***

Three days later, the crew aboard the *Lady Caroline* hoisted anchor and raised sail, headed for Charlestown, leaving the slaves behind, all except Alicia, her mother and the baby. In their place in the hold of the ship were barrels of molasses and locally made rum, called *cruzan* after the island of its origin.

Without the slaves to feed, and with a crew reduced by four, Fiona's task in the galley was far more manageable. They now had fresh water and had also taken on some new fruit she'd never seen before. They were called banana figs, curious-looking yellow things, like fat fingers. Alicia knew what to do with them instantly. She simply peeled and ate one, grinned, and handed another to Fiona, who took it cautiously and did the same. Sweet and delicious! Danny and Alicia's mother each tried one, and suddenly everyone's tears abated. Even the baby quieted, as if sensing his mother's feelings had calmed.

Sailing with just two masts crippled their journey, and Fiona saw the captain and Mr. Greene frequently scanning the horizon. "Watchin' out for pirates," Mr. Bearden told her. "With our ship damaged, we'd have little chance of outrunning them, but perhaps we could change course if we spied them first, and they didn't see us."

Fiona had overheard the sailors talking about pirates, and they'd even sung about them, but she hadn't thought of them as being a real threat. "What would happen if the pirates come?" she asked him.

"Ah, well, then, we'll all be deaded, for sure." Mr. Bearden said this with a laugh, but Fiona didn't find it funny.

"I didn't come all this way to be 'deaded,' Mr. Bearden. I hope you are wrong about that. I just want to get to Charlestown and off this ship!"

Bearden sighed. "Don't we all, lass? Don't we all?"

* * *

The dreaded pirates never appeared, and the *Lady Caroline* made its way into Charlestown harbor in early September. The captain had told Fiona that her indenture had been promised to a Major Stainton. "What is he like, if I may be so bold as to ask?" Fiona said.

The captain grinned. "Boldness has never been a problem for you," he laughed, then continued. "I've only met him once. He is a very wealthy and powerful man in Charlestown. A merchant and also a plantation owner. I asked around about him a bit after he solicited me to find a lady's maid for his wife. Seems he married his wealth. His wife, the former Beatrice Hamilton, is the daughter of an English earl, and her dowry included at least a thousand acres of the low country land nearby Charlestown."

Fiona let this sink in. She would be serving an English earl's daughter. It was an English earl who had so cruelly raised the rents of the tenant farmers who'd been her neighbors, forcing them to leave or starve. An earl who'd threatened to ship young Irish people like herself off as slaves, a threat that had brought her to this time and place. "Is... is she a nice person?" she managed.

"I have no idea what either of them is like, other than Stainton seemed rather pompous to me." He turned to Fiona and added, "I would never say that to anyone, however, and you shan't either," he warned. "He did tell me that Mrs. Stainton won't abide having an African as her personal servant, although they serve in the house. Apparently, she complained so bitterly to him that he asked me to find an appropriate indentured white girl to satisfy her and," he laughed, "to shut her up."

***

Eager to get a first look at the city that one if not both would soon call home, Fiona and Danny ran to the bow and clung to the rail as the ship approached. Fiona's heart pounded. What lay in store for her here? She recalled the tea leaves and the message that she would have many journeys in her future. Her sea journey was nearly over; what journeys could she possibly have on land?

While the sailors secured the ship at anchor, Fiona went below into the tiny cabin she'd called home for nearly three months. It smelled of unwashed people and clothing. She took out a small mirror and was horrified by her image. Her face was ruddy from the sun, her hair wild and looking as if it were on fire. Certainly, no lady's maid would look like this!

Taking no heed now of the need to preserve fresh water, she heated a pot on the cook stove and did her best to cleanse herself and her clothing. She donned the one dress she'd saved for her arrival, enjoying the feeling of freshness. She was just completing her grooming when Captain Michael came down the steps into the galley. He paused when he saw her, and then rewarded her with a warm smile. "You look very nice, Fiona," he said.

"Thank you, sir. I didn't realize what a fright I must have looked. I didn't want to meet Major Stainton like that."

"Very wise of you. But we'll not be taking you ashore right away. The ship will remain at anchor for some time. We've been forbidden to go into the docks."

"Forbidden? But why?"

"I understand that slave ships are quarantined until it is determined that we're bringing in no diseases. Also," he raised an eyebrow, "I heard they don't like ships in the dock area that stink."

Fiona couldn't suppress a smile. Yes, their ship did stink. "So how long do you reckon it will be?" She'd made the ocean passage and arrived alive. She was now anxious to get back on solid ground.

"I will go in tomorrow and make arrangements to meet Major Stainton. In the meantime, you will need to continue to prepare meals for the crew. And after tonight's meal, would you honor us with your company, and your fiddle, on the foredeck for what might be our last night of music?"

"It would be my honor, sir. And Danny?"

"Of course, bring him. But the darkies, well, they must stay below. They will be moved into town as soon as possible as well. But it is best they stay under guard until then lest they attempt to run away."

Fiona thought it highly unlikely Alicia and her mother would jump ship with a new baby, and they likely couldn't swim, but she recalled a man who had tried to drown himself when he was being hauled aboard from the longboat, and she didn't argue with the captain.

The music on board that night was bittersweet for Fiona. Oddly, she'd grown fond of many of the rough sailors whose voices joined in hearty song and who danced a lively jig to many of her fiddle tunes. Danny had practiced playing the wooden flute, and although he was not as accomplished as Mr. Bentley had been, he added a merry touch to the music making.

The following day, Captain Michael went ashore in the longboat, and upon his return mid-afternoon, he came to the galley. His face was flushed and his eyes brittle and bright, telltale signs he'd found a local pub. But Fiona didn't blame him. He deserved his drink after this voyage.

"I've met with Stainton; he's expecting us tomorrow. We're to meet him at the docks mid-day. In the meantime, I need you to prepare the women," he said. "Wash them and grease them with palm oil. They're all I have left to sell, so they must look their best. They shine when oiled."

Fiona was horrified. These people had been treated like animals for the most part, and only now allowed to be cleaned up. Made ready for sale!

Chapter Fifteen

Fiona arrived in Charlestown with Captain Michael shortly before noon on a hot September day, stepping foot on dry land for the first time in many weeks. She carried everything she owned in the small woolen satchel she'd brought from home. Happy as she was to have survived the grueling and emotional journey, new apprehensions attacked her. What would happen next?

"Wait here," the captain told her as he helped her out of the longboat onto the quay. "I will locate Stainton and come back for you."

Behind her, others of the ship's crew moved Alicia and her mother, clutching the baby, from a second boat onto the shore. Fiona had oiled them as instructed, and the ebony skin of the trio glistened in the sun. Fiona was ashamed for the role she had played in enabling the sale of human beings. Despite being warned against it, she'd grown fond of these people, and she wondered if she'd ever see them again.

Danny had chosen to remain behind and continue his life as a sailor. He had no prospect on shore, he told her. He'd be a beggar like before, and he had no taste for becoming indentured. "Besides," he remarked with a smile as they bid their farewells, "I'm a fair cook now. Been trained by the best!"

Fiona couldn't disagree with his reasoning, but she would miss him. As a parting gift, she handed him Mr. Bentley's flute. "You've become a right fair player, too," she grinned. "Keep it up and play a jig for the crew every night. Makes them happy!"

Captain Michael returned with Major Nigel Stainton, a military officer in the Queen's service. He was a stout man, broad and barrel-chested, dressed in civilian clothing of elegant style—white satin waistcoat with gold buttons, red woolen coat, and black breeches atop white stockings and black shoes. On his head, a white wig was crowned with a black tricorn. From his waist pocket hung a large gold watch. His face was ruddy, his eyes blue, and his demeanor not altogether pleasant. A line ran between his light blond brows, giving him the look of a permanent frown. His chin was weak and sloped into a short neck. She noticed he had very short fingers on his pudgy hands.

Fiona instinctively disliked him.

A second man approached and stood slightly behind Stainton. He was dressed in plain trousers and collarless shirt of white muslin, and his features were most peculiar. His skin was the color of tea, his dark eyes slanted above high cheekbones. He didn't look at all like the Africans whose skin was black and eyes large and round. Was he one of those Indians she'd heard about?

The captain took Fiona by the shoulders and brought her in front of him. "Major Stainton, this is the young woman we have spoken about, brought under indenture to serve as your wife's lady's maid," the captain said, as if presenting valuable goods.

Stainton's frown deepened. "Are you sure this is the one? I was expecting someone, well, larger in body."

All three men looked at Fiona with appraising eyes, and she wanted to disappear into the hot air. Instead she raised her chin. "You mean fat?" she retorted.

Stainton blinked at her insubordination. "You will not address me," he barked, then turned to the captain. "Where is she from?"

"Ulster, sir. Picked her up in Londonderry. She's been our ship's cook for the entire voyage. She is slight of build, but I can vouch for her work and her tenacity."

"I don't need tenacity," the major growled. "I want obedience." He turned back to Fiona. "Do you understand?" he said. "If I conclude my business here with Captain Michael, you will belong to me, for five years...if you behave. I demand obedience as well as service."

Fiona wanted to spit at his shiny black shoes, but instead held his gaze steadily. "You will get your money's worth, sir. But I was told the term was three years."

She saw the major's face grow red. "Then you were told wrongly. And keep your mouth shut!"

She felt Captain Michael squeeze her shoulders slightly, a signal to hold her tongue. But he had told her three years. Surely, he wouldn't renege on that now. He released his grip and withdrew a paper from his coat, opened it and read aloud: "It is here in the agreement we signed when last we met, sir," the captain said. "It says distinctly: *'This indenture is for and during the full Space, Time and Term of three Years from the first Day of the said servant's arrival in Charlestown in AMERICA, during which Time or Term the said Master or his Assigns shall and will find and supply the said servant with sufficient Meat, Drink, Apparel, Lodging and all other necessaries befitting such a Servant, and at the end and expiration of said Term, the said servant to be made Free, and received according to the Custom of the Country. The captain of the ship bearing the servant is to be paid 15 pounds upon delivery.'* It is signed, sir, by you."

"Fifteen pounds! Ridiculous! I never agreed to any such thing. I will not pay such a high ransom."

Now it was the captain's turn to grow red-faced. "Then, sir, we have no deal. I have in good faith and according to this contract brought and delivered an able-bodied, intelligent young woman to be your wife's lady's maid. If you do not wish to honor your contract, then we shall be off. I am certain I can find another master in the Virginia colony who will see the value of this servant." He paused, then eyed the major shrewdly. "I wouldn't want to be the one to tell your wife she's to have no lady's maid, now that she's expecting her to arrive today."

Fiona thought Major Stainton would explode. It was obvious he was unused to being challenged. She made a mental note of that. She didn't want to go with him, and silently hoped he would back out on his agreement to purchase her indenture. But in the end, he agreed to a three-year term and fifteen pounds. "Robbery," he grumbled, then turned to her. "Obedience, do you understand? You are to obey my wife, and myself as well, to fulfill the contract for three years."

"I understand, sir," she said meekly, fearing he might strike her if she said anything else cheeky. Three years loomed like a dark cloud on her horizon.

That transaction agreed upon, Captain Michael then offered Stainton the opportunity to purchase Alicia and her mother. She wondered briefly if he did this to please her, knowing as he did she'd been protective of them on board, or if it was just convenient to have a potential buyer to take them quickly off his hands.

"They are all the Africans I have left," he said. "Sold the others for a handsome profit on Saint Croix. These weren't available at the time, the mother having just given birth and all."

They moved to a large, fenced holding area, unprotected from the harsh southern sun. where Alicia and her mother huddled against a wall. "Women. I don't particularly need any more women at Edgewater," Stainton said brusquely, apparently still miffed at not being able to negotiate a better deal for Fiona.

"Ah, but I can give you three for the price of two," the captain replied. "The baby, which is a boy, comes free."

Stainton considered this a moment. "Yes, but it's going to be years before he can be useful in the fields." He turned to the other man who had followed them silently. "Wouldn't you say, Locksley?"

Fiona surmised that this man he called Locksley was Stainton's slave and would agree to anything his master said. But before he could reply, the captain went on.

"Yes, but he's yours for no cost. You'll get a young, strong boy in a few years, at no investment other than to keep him alive."

Again, Stainton looked to Locksley, who said nothing, but shrugged his shoulders and nodded, as if indifferent. Stainton turned back to Captain Michael. "So, what's your exorbitant price for them?"

Captain Michael named a price so low even Fiona couldn't believe it, but her guess had been correct, that he just wanted to be rid of them. He'd told her he wanted the wretched business behind him and that he wasn't going to undertake slaving ever again. She recognized again that in his own way, the captain was a man of integrity.

Stainton gave orders to Locksley to fetch the newly purchased slaves. "Take them in your wagon back to Edgewater and find a place for them in the slave village. I have other business to attend to here. I shall return in time for tea."

Now the time had come that Fiona had both anticipated and feared.

She bade a bittersweet goodbye to Captain Michael, scarcely able to hold back her tears. "May you have fair winds, Captain," she said. "And no hurricanes."

To her surprise, the captain took her hand and kissed her fingers. "And to you, Miss Fiona, a safe and prosperous new life in America."

CHAPTER SIXTEEN

After the captain headed back to his ship, Major Stainton turned to Fiona. "That dress is dreadful," he remarked. "And you smell bad. I cannot take you to Beatrice in this condition."

"'Tis the best I have, sir," she replied, half offended, half embarrassed.

"Well, *'t'isnt* good enough," he snapped, mocking her Irish accent. They boarded his large, handsome carriage; as they rode over the rough city streets, Fiona leaned out the window, unabashedly taking in the bustle of this New World city. It was far different from Liverpool, drenched in sunlight and with wider streets. Still, like Liverpool, it smelled of horse dung, made pungent as it roasted in the sun.

Their destination was a grand house on a side street in the center of town. Stainton stepped from the carriage and headed toward the front door without looking back. Fiona hesitated at the carriage door, unsure what was expected of her. Almost to the entrance, Stainton at last turned back to her. "Well, come along," he said impatiently, beckoning her with his hand. "Come!"

Fiona left her satchel in the carriage and dashed to catch up with him and did so just as the door swung open into the most beautiful room she had ever seen. A crystal chandelier hung above a large entryway, and a grand curved staircase led to the upper floor. A woman dressed in an elegant silken gown that appeared to be made of spun gold greeted the major with a gracious bow.

"Nigel! How good to see you. It has been awhile."

The major cleared his throat. "Yes, Floretta. Business on the plantation, you know. I must make a point to come into Charlestown more often."

Fiona saw the woman smile flirtatiously. "We always welcome you here, sir. What may we do for you today?"

Major Stainton pushed Fiona forward with a shove. "I need you to make her decent," he said. "She's fresh off a ship, a slave ship I might add," he remarked with meaning. "Smells to high heaven. She's to be Beatrice's lady's maid. Can you clean her up? Get her a decent dress? Not one that's too expensive, mind you."

"Consider it done." Floretta called to someone in an adjacent room, and a young woman in an equally beautiful blue gown appeared. Fiona noticed both of their gowns were very low cut in the front, showing ample expanses of lily-white bosoms. Floretta spoke to the girl.

"Major Stainton has a request, Rose," she said, and brushed her arm in Fiona's direction. "This girl is in need of...repair. She needs a bath, and scent, and a new garment. May I commend her to your attention?" Her smile seemed forced. "I'm sure the Major will make it worth our while," she added sweetly.

Rose glared at Fiona. She obviously wasn't used to cleaning up rough Irish servant girls. But she made no argument. "But of course, Madam," was all she said, then indicated for Fiona to follow her.

As they left, she heard Floretta say to the Major, "And now, sir, I hope there is something special I can do for you."

Chapter Seventeen

Two hours later, Fiona was presented in her new finery to the man who now owned her, or at least her services, for the next three years. She had to admit she enjoyed the long soak in the tin tub, but she was revolted by the cloying scent of the perfume Rose insisted she must wear.

Her new dress was nicer than any she had ever owned, but nothing to compare to those of the ladies in this house. It was made of cotton, with a tiny rosebud print on the fabric. It buttoned high on her neck and had a white lace collar.

Rose had taken great pains to try to tame Fiona's wild hair. After washing it, she rubbed it with a rich scented oil, thinking that would ease the curls, but it only managed to make them oily curls.

"Your hair's like a nigger's," she grouched. "Where'd you get these frizzy locks?"

Fiona was shocked and offended. "From my own people. In Ireland. We're from a long line of ginger hairs. My Granny told me it comes from the far north countries."

"Well, if I was you, I'd cut it clean off and start over."

In the end, Rose allowed Fiona to brush her own hair, and they tied it as neatly as possible with a ribbon at the nape of her neck. Rose pinched Fiona's cheeks, "to raise some color," she explained.

The reflection in the cheval mirror showed a slender girl in a modest dress, with hair tied out of the way, and a new pair of slippers on her feet. Fiona swallowed hard. She couldn't help but like what she saw, although she wasn't particularly fond of the way she'd been handled by Rose. Still, she turned to the other woman. "Thank you," she said quietly.

When they returned to the entry hall, Rose said, "Wait here," indicating a low bench along one wall. And then she left.

Shortly, Major Stainton came into the hall, accompanied by Floretta. His wig was askew and his clothing disheveled. However, he looked a bit more serene than he had when they first arrived. "Stand up, girl," he ordered, looking at her appraisingly. "Yes, yes, much better. Beatrice should be pleased." He turned to Floretta. "Put this on my bill."

And with that, he exited the grand front door and headed for his carriage. Fiona looked around to see if either Floretta or Rose were about to give her further instructions, but the hall was empty now except for herself, so she followed her new master out the door and into the carriage. Much like a loyal dog, she thought, disgusted at herself but knowing there was no option.

The major instructed the horseman to stop next at a large wooden warehouse fronted by an open-air market where he stepped down from the carriage and walked toward a group of men unlike any Fiona had ever seen. Their skin was red-brown, marked with dark, strange symbols. Their heads were shaved, with only a spike of hair at the crest, festooned with feathers. Their upper bodies were bare except for some necklaces and arm bands, and they wore leggings of animal skins atop soft shoes of some sort. Beaded and metal ornaments hung from their ear lobes. Fiona's heart pounded. Who were these people? They were different from the Africans, but similar in that they appeared very primitive. Neither did they look at all like Locksley.

Maybe *these* were the Indians she'd heard Captain Michael and the others speak of.

She watched as the major approached the group and saw a rough-looking white man step from behind the Indians. "So, Stainton, where're the guns?" He carried a long rifle, and his clothes were filthy.

"Show me the pelts first, McNeill," the major replied evenly. The two men talked in voices too low for her to hear, then they turned abruptly and walked into the warehouse building, and Fiona lost sight of them. Curiosity overcame caution, and quietly she let herself out of the carriage and followed them. The colorful band of Indians stood silently by, their only apparent notice of her in the glance of their eyes. She was afraid, but they seemed harmless enough.

Inside the warehouse, which adjoined the wharf, she saw large crates she recognized as being similar to those containing the guns Captain Michael had delivered to the slave agent in Africa. There were barrels as well, and she overheard Major Stainton bargaining with the white man.

"I never promised you one hundred, and certainly cannot deliver that number with the puny load of furs you're offering," he scoffed. It reminded her of how he'd tried to cheat Captain Michael regarding her indenture.

"Puny!" The white man exploded. "You're a thief, Stainton, and I'm tired of dealin' with ya."

"Who else are you going to sell to, McNeill? You know as well as I do there's not another merchant in Charlestown who can rid you of those hides for any better price than I'm offering. Those redskins would as soon have your scalp as leave here without their guns." He paused, then continued. "Tell you what, I'll give you sixty guns and a barrel of whiskey for those pelts."

The man named McNeill walked away, then came back again. "Eighty guns. And two barrels."

Stainton held his ground. "Sixty. No more."

At that, McNeill strode off, returning to the small group of Indians. He passed right by her without seeing her, but she tucked herself away in the shadows, expecting Major Stainton to return as well. But he did not.

In a few moments, McNeill came back, followed by the Indians, one of which held a long knife alongside one leg. Without a word, the savages surrounded Stainton, and two of them seized his arms. The one wielding the knife threw the major's wig onto the floor and grabbed him by his thick blond hair. Stainton shouted, "Stop it! No! Call them off, McNeill!"

"So, now what do you say, you crooked, lying, cheating thief?" McNeill confronted him. "The guns, or your scalp. One hundred guns, and three barrels of whiskey."

Fiona had never been so frightened in her life. Would they really cut his scalp away? "All right," Stainton bellowed, floundering to try to get loose. "No need to get violent. It's not the way real men do business."

"These *are* the real men," McNeill sneered, indicating the Indians. "The ones you don't want to mess with. Or cheat. Now, I suggest you lead us to our rightful due, and we shall in turn provide you with some of the finest hides and pelts available from the high mountains of this fair land."

Fiona didn't wait to hear more but ran as fast as she could back to the carriage, climbed in and slammed the door. She didn't care if the horseman heard her, although she was sure Stainton would be furious to learn she'd witnessed the ugly proceedings.

Within half an hour, Major Stainton strode back to the carriage, his face scarlet but his hair intact. He carried the wig in one hand and a piece of paper in the other. Upon reaching the carriage, he looked at his large gold watch. Then he shouted up at the driver, "On, Winston, we're late." He swung his bulk up into the carriage just as the driver set it in motion, settled the wig back onto his head, and wiped his face with a linen handkerchief.

Fiona sat as far away from him as possible in the small space and kept her mouth shut. She saw him take a small flask from one of his pockets and draw deeply on it. This seemed to settle him a bit, and only after a few moments did he seem to realize she was there.

"What are you staring at?" he growled.

Fiona hadn't realized she was staring, but she was. This big, brash man looked totally undone. "I'm sorry, sir. I didn't mean to. It's only..."

"Only what?"

"Only that, well, you look a fright."

He glared at her. "And who are you to tell me how I look, you impudent little slut?"

Fiona was incensed. "I am no slut, sir. I was just trying to return a favor."

He frowned. "What favor?"

"You provided me with a bath and new clothing, sir, so that I would be presentable to your wife. I was only going to suggest you straighten your wig on our journey, and..." she paused, hesitating with her next suggestion.

"And?" he said impatiently.

"And, well, sir, you might want to button your breeches."

Chapter Eighteen

Edgewater Plantation, South Carolina, August 1751

Edgewater was aptly named, as Fiona was later to learn, because the plantation lay at the banks of the lazily flowing Ashley River. As they approached the house on a long, tree-lined drive, again Fiona shamelessly peered from the carriage window. The trees along the lane appeared to be young, but elsewhere on the expansive lawn were large, strange-looking trees, stout and gnarly. From their dark green foliage hung some kind of peculiar, gray-green decoration in an eerie disarray that put her distinctly ill at ease.

At the far end of the drive stood a large, white two-story house. A set of steps led up to the main entrance, which was elevated from the ground level, and long verandahs stretched across the width of the house on both floors. Above, a slanted roof met at a point in the center. Two chimneys stood guard on each side of the house. She drew in a sharp breath. This place was different from the house in Charlestown, not as elegant, but still more house than she'd ever known.

One black serving woman and the exotic looking Locksley awaited their arrival, along with a very short, stout, and dour-looking woman in a handsome dress made of a deep purple fabric. Fiona heard Stainton let out a long sigh. "Maybe I should have stayed the night at Floretta's," he muttered under his breath. Then to her he said, "Stay here. I'll fetch you in a minute."

He stepped from the carriage and went to the little woman. "Beatrice, my dear. I have brought you a present. I hope you will be pleased."

"As long as she's not a darkie, Nigel. You promised…"

"And I have delivered." He looked back at the carriage. "Fiona! You can come now. I want you to meet your new mistress."

Fiona felt all eyes on her as she clambered down from the carriage clutching her satchel and walked toward the assembly. She was filled with apprehension and her heart was pounding, but she held her head high and her gaze steady. When she reached the woman, Beatrice, her new mistress, she gave a quick curtsey. "Pleased to meet you, madam."

Her courtesy was not returned. Instead, Beatrice Stainton glared at her. "You're a thin little thing," was all she said. "With terrible hair. Nigel," she snapped, turning back to her husband. "Where on earth did you find this thing?"

Nigel Stainton straightened and returned Beatrice's glare with equal enmity, and Fiona knew in a flash this wasn't a happy household. "This 'thing,' as you call her, is Fiona Cassidy, come from Ulster, Ireland, aboard a reputable ship. The captain has assured me she is sound and works well. Seems she had to serve as the ship's cook on the voyage. That should prove her worth to you as a servant, my dear. She is yours for...three years."

Beatrice sniffed. "I don't need a cook. I need a lady's maid." Then she sighed. "Well, at least she's white, even if she's Irish. If this is the best you can find, I guess she will have to do." With that, she turned, climbed awkwardly up the steps, and disappeared through the large front doors. Fiona noticed she had an odd gait.

Stainton indicated for Fiona to follow her, but he didn't accompany them. Instead, he turned to Locksley. "Come with me," she heard him command, and she watched as the pair headed toward a nearby building, the major striding ahead of his servant.

Inside the house, the air was much cooler, and it took a moment for Fiona's eyes to adjust to the dim light. When they did, she saw Beatrice seated on a short bench in the long hallway that appeared to run the length of the house, eyeing her speculatively. "What did he say your name is?" she asked in a sharp tone.

"Fiona. Fiona Cassidy, madam."

"Don't call me madam," Beatrice said. "That's Floretta's job."

Fiona raised her eyebrows. "You know Floretta?"

Beatrice laughed scornfully. "I know everything, child, and don't you forget it. I know where Nigel goes when he's in Charlestown. I have my spies. Floretta's whorehouse. I daresay that's where you've been as well, am I right?"

Fiona's apprehension suddenly turned to nausea. She feared betraying Stainton, but she was no liar. "Major Stainton took me there, my lady, to, uh, clean me up. You see, I'd been on board a ship for months, and I wasn't, well, presentable."

"My lady? Well, that's better. I am a lady, you know. Or once was, until I was sent off to this miserable hell hole to become nothing more than a farmer's wife."

Fiona managed to keep her face expressionless, not knowing how to take this tiny woman's vitriol. "Shall I call you m'lady, or Lady Stainton?"

Beatrice's expression softened slightly. "Both. Depending on the circumstances. Now, I won't have you here in those clothes from the brothel. I will have Locksley return to my special resource in Charlestown to acquire more suitable attire for you. What have you in there?" she asked, pointing to the grubby satchel.

"My belongings, my lady, as meagre as they are."

"Well, let me see them," she demanded, holding out her small hand.

Fiona dared not cross her new mistress, so she placed the satchel on the gleaming wooden floor, knelt, and opened it. She drew out the bloodstained nightgown, two undergarments, her well-worn dress, and her few items for personal grooming.

Beatrice made a face. "Disgusting! But I guess it's to be expected of the low Irish. I want you to throw these garments out as soon as Locksley returns. I will provide you with attire befitting a proper lady's maid." Then she spied something else in the satchel. "What's that?"

Fiona's hand trembled as she withdrew her father's fiddle. "'Tis my fiddle, m'lady. Given me by my Da when I left."

"Fiddle? Don't you mean violin?"

Fiona grinned. "'Tis very much like that other instrument, m'lady, but not exactly. We played it for dancin' at our *ceilidh*, you see." Her fingers itched to play it now, for anytime she touched it, she felt a little closer to home again.

"Well, I don't know what you're talking about, but I have no wish to have peasant music in my home, so unless you can play something of the classical nature, please refrain from playing it at all."

At this, Fiona replaced the instrument in the satchel, atop the other items—her notebooks and herbs that had made the long voyage with her, and the talisman stone. Surely, she was to be allowed to have something of her very own here.

Beatrice led Fiona to her quarters which were at the rear of the house, overlooking some outbuildings and a number of small huts that reminded her of the farmers' cottages in Ireland, except they were made of rough wood instead of stone and faded gray with the weather. It was a small room but much larger than her tiny space on board the ship, and she was grateful for the window that let in plenty of light. The furnishings were modest but clean—a narrow bed set against one wall, a small dresser with a mirror, an upright cabinet of some sort, and a chest upon which was a ceramic pitcher and bowl. She spied a chamber pot by the side of the bed. The floor was bare. She turned to Beatrice.

"This is very nice, m'lady. I thank you."

It was only then that Beatrice pointed out a door on one inner wall. "It'll be convenient at any rate," she said, hobbling to the door and throwing it open with a bang. "Follow me."

On the other side of the doorway was a much larger room, lavishly furnished and decorated. "This is my chamber," Beatrice informed her. "And this," she said, picking up a large bell, "is how you will know when I am in need of you." She rang it sharply, and Fiona winced at the reverberating sound. "I will ring for you, and you are to come at once, do you understand?"

Fiona nodded, wondering if she was to remain in her room at all times when she wasn't needed to serve her mistress, knowing if this was so, she would go mad. "May I ask, m'lady, what services I am to provide you?"

At that Beatrice looked perplexed, then sighed. "I guess I can't expect you to know the duties of a lady's maid. Doubt if they have such a thing in Ireland. Well, if we were in England," she continued, sounding more than a little annoyed, "it might be to help me dress for the formal dinners I knew at Ensley Hall. But here, we have no such social life. Still, I have need of assistance with dressing." She plopped down onto the bench in front of her elaborate dressing table. "I'm sure you must have noticed by now that I have trouble walking. That is why my quarters are on this floor instead of upstairs with the other chambers."

Fiona didn't reply, because she didn't know what to say. A long silence ensued, then Beatrice looked up at Fiona. "I am an aberration of nature, Fiona," she said abruptly, startling Fiona with her frankness. "Here, see for yourself. You might as well know, since you're to be my lady's maid." With that she hitched up her long skirt to reveal short, misshapen legs, and feet that turned inward. "I was born this way. My father never wanted me to live, especially since my mother died giving birth to me. He tolerated me, but until I reached young womanhood, he mostly kept me out of sight. Clearly to him, I was a disgrace to the family."

The bitterness in her voice and the tears brimming in her eyes caught Fiona's heart. "I...I am sorry to hear of it, m'lady," she said.

Beatrice gathered herself together again and went on. "But he couldn't exactly get rid of me," she continued in a cold tone. "Too many knew about me, and about my condition. Some, including my mother's sister, were actually kind to me once in a while. It was she who suggested to my father the answer to his problem—give me a handsome dowry and marry me off. And so he did."

She stood up again and moved to one of her windows that overlooked the gardens. She continued without looking back at Fiona. "I have never told this to anyone," she confided. "Why I am telling you now I do not know. There's something about you..."

"I will keep your trust, m'lady, but it will help me to serve you better to know...uh, how things are for you."

"You will keep my trust," she said, turning and looking straight at Fiona, "or you will die."

Fiona suddenly wondered if this woman was mad, or a murderer, or what? She stood speechless until Beatrice resumed. "I don't mean that, of course. But there is more you should know about this godforsaken household if you are to be part of it for the next three years. But first, I must ring for tea. I fear this has all been rather much for me."

She pulled a long strip of embroidered tapestry that hung by her bedside, and shortly one of the black servants who had been in front to greet Fiona appeared with a tray holding a silver tea service and a plate of small sandwiches. She placed the tray on a low table that sat between two armchairs, then silently withdrew.

"That was Eliza," Beatrice said, taking a seat in one of the chairs but not inviting Fiona to sit. She poured one cup of tea and added cream and lumps of sugar, but she did not offer tea to Fiona. Only as she watched her new mistress eat did Fiona realize how hungry she was. It had been a long time since her farewell breakfast on board the *Lady Caroline*, and she'd been offered nothing to eat since.

"She's a good nigger but not real bright," Beatrice continued after consuming two of the sandwiches. "Wish I could find someone better to cook for us."

"I can cook, m'lady," Fiona offered, thinking if she had work to do in the kitchen, at least she'd find something to eat.

"Oh, no. That won't do. A lady's maid does not cook, Fiona."

What if a lady's maid starves before she can serve the lady, Fiona thought, but held her tongue.

Beatrice continued. "I'm only going to tell you this once, Fiona. Beware of Nigel. He's a good-for-nothing toady who saw my dowry as his way out of his poor prospects as the second son of a penurious baronet. He married me, crippled girl that I am, in exchange for a land grant of a thousand acres, which is now this plantation, the military title of Major, and five thousand pounds. His only promise, other than the standard marriage vows which he has never found sacred or binding, was to take me away from England and never return." She set her teacup down with a clatter. "My warning to you is, stay away from him. He has a *penchant* for pursuing young women, and to him, you will be fresh game."

CHAPTER NINETEEN

Later, Fiona helped Beatrice change into evening attire for dinner, which tradition, she learned, was the lady's pathetic attempt to hold on to some semblance of her former aristocratic life. She followed her mistress into the dining room and seated her as she was directed at one end of a long table. There was but a single place set for dinner. Fiona wondered if the major had returned to Floretta's.

"You may go now," Beatrice said to Fiona. "You are to take your meals in the kitchen, but you are not to eat with the niggers." She sniffed, then added, "I will find my way back to my quarters after dinner."

Fiona left Beatrice to her solitary dinner and returned to her room to settle in. Her stomach growled, however, and she decided that finding the kitchen and some dinner held priority. Peering out of her window, she saw a covered walkway that led from the rear of the big house to a brick structure, and she caught a glimpse through the open doorway of Eliza moving about inside. Tiptoeing across the hall and out the rear door, she quickly traversed the short distance to the brick structure and was rewarded by the smell of food cooking.

When she entered the kitchen, Eliza looked up at her and backed away. "Missy, no mean no trouble."

"Trouble?" Fiona frowned, then saw that the woman was afraid of her. She smiled to ease Eliza's fear. "No trouble, Eliza. Just hungry. Lady Beatrice said I could take my dinner here."

Eliza pointed to a large pot on the cook stove. "*Purloo* on the stove, Missy."

Fiona had no idea what *purloo* was; she crossed the room and peered into the pot. A mix of rice and some reddish-purple peas were steamed together in the deep container. The peas reminded Fiona of the horse peas they'd brought from Africa on the ship only they were lighter in color. Eliza approached her and spooned a heaping mound of the mixture into a large ceramic bowl and handed it to Fiona. Without another word, she pointed to a table on the far side of the room and gave Fiona a fork and spoon. She looked quizzically at Fiona for a quick second, and then dashed out of the back of the kitchen house.

The *purloo* tasted wonderful, because not only was Fiona ravenous, it was also cooked with bacon that was a deep red in color and more flavorful than any she'd ever eaten. Her hunger satisfied, she returned to her room and stood for a long time gazing out of the tall window.

Daylight was fading, but she could see flat fields stretching from the far side of the small houses down almost to the river. The fields themselves appeared to be underwater because they reflected the golden glint of sunset on the clouds. What was it they grew here?

Fiona set about unpacking, removing all except the fiddle from the satchel, which she stashed beneath the bed. She hung her shabby dress and the clean but stained nightgown on a hook and slipped the talisman stone beneath her pillow. She put her notebooks, herbs, and toiletries into the shallow drawers of the dressing table, then eyed herself in the mirror.

The girl she saw there wasn't the girl who'd left Ireland in the spring. Her skin was roughened from the sun and sea wind. Her eyes looked older, somehow sad even when she ventured a small smile. And then, for a fleeting moment, the image of her Granny flickered briefly across her own face. "Granny," she whispered, and reached out to touch the mirror. The image vanished, but Fiona was sure it had been her Granny reaching out to her, giving her courage. She swallowed over a slight lump in her throat and turned away to look out of the window again.

Outside she saw a group of the Africans who worked on this plantation moving toward the center of the cluster of small houses, and she wondered if Alicia and her mother were among them. She wanted to go to them, but suddenly she heard the harsh bell summoning her to Beatrice's service.

She knocked on the door that connected their chambers, opened it tentatively and said, "Yes, m'lady?"

Beatrice was seated at her dressing table. "I'm tired. I want to go to bed."

"Yes, m'lady." Fiona approached the little woman and felt a deep sorrow for her. Where was her husband? She obviously had no children. It occurred to her that Beatrice Stainton, for all her title and wealth, had no one.

Beatrice directed Fiona to a large wardrobe, instructed her on which garment she wished to wear for sleeping, and said little more. Silently, Fiona helped her change, then picked up a silver handled hairbrush that lay on the dresser. "May I, m'lady?"

At first Beatrice didn't understand. "May you what?"

"Brush your hair, m'lady. I like to brush mine before retiring, it stimulates the scalp and aids sleep."

Beatrice looked up at Fiona's thick, red hair. "Humph," she snorted. "I'm surprised you can get a brush through those weeds."

Fiona chose to laugh rather than take offense, because what she said was true. "Yes, m'lady. I have to use a very stiff brush."

At that, Beatrice also gave a small laugh. "Very well."

The woman's hair was dark, accented with silver strands, and when let down from her severe style, fell in soft waves over her shoulders. Fiona found it even silky to the touch, and she looked at Beatrice in the mirror as she brushed. The woman's face had lost its harshness, and in the light of the candle lanterns, she looked much younger. Fiona wondered how old she was but didn't dare ask. Instead, she said, "Does that feel all right, m'lady?"

Beatrice actually smiled and closed her eyes. "Heavenly. I haven't had this pleasure since I left Ensley Hall. I hope you are correct in saying it aids sleep. I have difficulty at night, first falling asleep, then staying asleep."

Fiona thought quickly, wondering if she dared offer a possible solution to her mistress's insomnia. "Have you tried chamomile tea, m'lady?"

"Tea! At night?"

"Yes, but not your regular kind of tea. This is an herbal brew that many times helps people relax and go to sleep."

Beatrice considered this. "And where does one get this, what did you call it?"

"Chamomile." During the long voyage, Fiona had used up the

supply Granny had given her, but it wasn't an uncommon herb. She was, in fact, surprised that Beatrice did not know of it. It might indeed grow wild here. "Perhaps we can find some in Charlestown. If we can find seeds, we might be able to grow it here. I saw you have a garden."

At that Beatrice brightened perceptively. "It is my only consolation for living here." She pointed to the window. "There, out there, is my garden. Locksley helps me keep it up."

It was nearly dark, but Fiona went to the window and could make out what appeared to be a formal garden, complete with a rose arbor. "Roses! Do you have roses?"

Beatrice preened. "Yes. I brought them from England. They have managed to survive despite the summer heat. And here I discovered something equally as beautiful that blooms in winter. Camellias. I will show you tomorrow."

Fiona at last managed to get Beatrice settled into her bed and blew out the candles. "Goodnight, m'lady," she whispered as she left.

She closed the door behind her, wondering if she dared take off now into the darkness to explore what she believed to be the slave quarters. From her window, she saw the glow of firelight coming from that direction and decided to take a chance. She wanted to know what fate had befallen Alicia and her mother.

The doors to the big house were unlocked, at least for the moment, and Fiona took the opportunity to slip out into the night. The air was soft, warm, unlike the sharp, damp, cold of late summer in Ireland. She paused at the edge of the kitchen house and heard the sound of singing, drumming, and some kind of instrument. Without another thought, she left the safety of the shadows and walked toward the firelight and the music.

She came upon a group of Africans gathered around a bonfire, singing and dancing. The women were dressed in bright clothing, the men in shirts and pantaloons. One man beat a rhythm on a dried gourd, while another strummed an instrument Fiona had never seen. It, too, appeared to be made from a gourd, cut in half and covered with some kind of animal skin. It was mounted to a long neck, much like the neck of her own fiddle, and a set of strings was stretched between the base of the gourd and the top of the neck. It made a plunking sort of sound. Two women held scarves in which they carried some kind of rattle that they shook in time to the music. The rest were dancing, singing, or both.

She was barely within the perimeter of the firelight when they spotted her, and the merriment immediately ceased. They stood and moved away almost as a single body, in fear of this white person who had appeared out of the night. From their ranks, a single figure made her way forward. She wore the traditional wound scarf headdress of the African style, and a clean, simple dress. Fiona recognized her immediately.

"Alicia!"

CHAPTER TWENTY

Fiona was overjoyed to learn that Alicia, her mother and baby brother had indeed been brought to Edgewater, and although they were enslaved, they appeared to have been treated well. Alicia looked relieved and comfortable among others like her. She turned and spoke to them in her native tongue, telling them they were safe with Fiona.

But then she turned and frowned at Fiona. "No stay here," she warned. "Not good for you. Not good for us."

"But..."

"No. People say boss woman no allow us with you."

Boss woman? Would they be speaking of Beatrice, who seemed loathe to have any contact with the black slaves on her plantation? Maybe Alicia meant boss man, Locksley or even Stainton.

"I will go," she said. "You and mama and *abofra*, the baby, alright?"

Alicia smiled and nodded. "Better than boat."

Fiona turned and headed back toward the house, sorry that she'd interrupted the evening for these people, but in a way, glad to know they had their music and their own kind to enjoy.

She wished the same for herself.

She was almost to the rear door when from out of the darkness a strong arm grabbed her by the shoulders and roughly turned her around.

"What're you doing snooping around here?"

Fiona looked up into the face of Locksley. "I...I saw a fire from my window. I went to see if something was burning down." It was a lie, but only a little one.

Locksley hustled her back into the big house. "You must not go out there again," he said in a hoarse whisper. "Lady Stainton holds no quarter with white folk being with the blacks."

So, she *was* the boss woman. Fiona recalled Nigel Stainton telling her that Beatrice would not abide having a negro servant as a lady's maid. "I meant no harm, sir," she said.

"Very well. But never go there again. The Staintons exact severe punishment for those who cross them."

Fiona had no doubt about that. But she wasn't going to promise what she might not be able to honor. "I understand," was all she said. "Mr. Locksley, if I may be so bold to inquire, what is your station here on the plantation?"

They were standing in the darkened hallway near the door to Fiona's room. Locksley motioned her to follow him, and they went through the house out onto the large front verandah. "We mustn't disturb the missus," he said. "She has trouble sleeping. To answer your question, I am the overseer of the plantation for Major Stainton, and...well, I also serve Lady Stainton's needs. At least I have until you arrived. I must say I will be glad to hand over some of those duties to you, hopefully." He sounded both wistful and doubtful.

Fiona found it curious that Beatrice would allow a man, especially a man of color, to serve her personal needs, but she didn't remark on that. "She told me you were to bring me new garments, as she doesn't want me wearing this," she indicated the dress from Floretta's place.

"Yes. I must return to Charlestown tomorrow for Major Stainton, and the lady has given me instructions to also go to her dressmaker there and have several items made up for you."

"Really? What items? And how will they know my size?"

"I helped her make a list," he said. "But as for size...I don't know."

"In regard to m'lady's problems with sleeping, I have suggested we find some chamomile to aid with that. I have none in my kit, but I would suspect we could find some in the market in Charlestown. Would it be possible for me to accompany you tomorrow to the dressmaker's? It would be much simpler for her to measure my size. And then we could perhaps find the tea makings I believe would be most helpful to Lady Stainton."

Locksley didn't speak right away. "I'm not sure that's a good idea, Miss Fiona," he said finally. "I have work to do for the major."

"You could leave me off at the dressmakers and go do your work. I can wait there until you come back for me," Fiona pleaded.

The man let out a long breath, then said, "We will have to ask Lady Stainton," but it was clear he did not like the idea.

Fiona did not want to alienate this man who might become an ally in this strange place, and so she said quietly, "If you do not wish me to go with you, I won't. It just seems the most efficient way to get things done."

He stood and went to the front steps. "I see. Well, we must get her permission in the morning. And now, I bid you goodnight, Miss Fiona Cassidy."

* * *

The next morning, after Fiona helped Beatrice into her day dress and watched her finish her breakfast, she approached her with her request to accompany Locksley into Charlestown. "I wish to acquire that tea we spoke of yesterday, and it seems to me that the dressmaker would have an easier time fitting my size if I was there for her to measure."

"Certainly not!" Beatrice said at first. "I...I need you here."

Fiona held her tongue and waited, silently folding a garment and returning it to Lady Stainton's closet. Moments later, Beatrice cleared her throat. "But I do suppose that makes sense," she admitted. "Locksley would have no idea how to find that tea, and I dearly want to try it."

"Very well, m'lady," Fiona said, scarcely able to suppress a grin. "I will make sure you have everything you need close at hand in my absence."

Permission thus granted, Fiona straightened Lady Stainton's chamber and did a few chores as she was bidden. At nine o'clock, she went to the front of the house to where she was to meet Locksley. His wagon and horse were there, but he was nowhere to be seen. Fiona went to the horse and stroked her nose, speaking to her in ancient Gaelic a charm that was said to enchant horses. The mare seemed to like it and gave a little whicker and nodded her head.

At that moment, Fiona saw Locksley coming out of the door of the stone building off to the side of the big house, followed by Stainton. Locksley did not look happy, nor did the major. Had she been the cause of some argument? Perhaps she should have asked permission of Stainton as well as his wife to go into Charlestown. She hoped she hadn't landed Locksley in some kind of trouble.

But neither said a word to her as Locksley approached. He indicated for her to mount the wagon but didn't offer to help her up. He went to the other side and plopped onto the hard, wooden seat beside her, took the reins, and snapped the horse into motion. Fiona dared not ask him what was wrong, and they rode in silence for a long while.

At last, Fiona risked conversation. "How long have you been at Edgewater, Mr. Locksley?" she asked, thinking this a safe enough topic. She was also curious to know more about this exotic looking man.

At first, he didn't reply, but eventually said, "Since before there was an Edgewater. More than a dozen years now, I figure." He said no more, but Fiona wasn't going to let it go at that.

"So, are you from here?"

He gave her a sideways look. "You always ask so many questions?"

She huffed. "I don't mean to be rude, Mr. Locksley, but I have been set upon this strange land and thrust into a job I am not sure I am up to. I...I'm just trying to find my way."

At that, he grinned. "That's the way it is with so many who come here, set here whether they wanted to be or not. You can call me Locksley. Don't need no 'mister.'"

Fiona smiled over at him and relaxed a little. "Thanks. I won't pry if you don't want to answer my questions," she said, waited a beat, then added, "but I do have many questions, and I would so appreciate your help."

Locksley didn't reply, just tweaked the reins and kept his eyes on the path. Fiona was unsure how, or if, she should proceed, but decided to push her luck. He hadn't thrown her off the cart yet. "So, were you sent here too, whether you wanted to come or not?"

"My grandpa was. Came as a slave on a brigantine from Madagascar. Story's been handed down and told many times so's I guess it's alright to tell it again." He leaned against the low backboard of the wagon and settled into his tale. "Ship was caught in a mighty storm, probably a hurricane, and came into Charlestown harbor for repair. Captain's name was Thurber. He came upon a local fellow, Henry Woodward, sort of a trader and deal-maker who knew a lot about the Indians and fancied one day becoming a planter hereabouts."

Fiona wasn't sure where he was going with this, and she noted that he was quite well- spoken. She said nothing, waiting for him to continue.

"That captain had brought rice from Madagascar, and story goes he gave a bag of it to Woodward, said it was the best rice in the world, and he was hoping it could be cultivated in the Virginia colony, where he was headed. Having no land himself, Woodward approached the manager of a big plantation owned by some earl, the Lord Proprietor."

Fiona was fascinated. She had no idea where Madagascar might be, or anything about rice, but she understood the Lord Proprietor thing. "So what happened?"

"Well, neither him or that manager knew anything about rice, so before the captain sailed again, Woodward went to him and bought my grandpa, who'd been raised on a rice plantation in Madagascar. Bought him and gave him an English name, Robert Locksley, and it was him, my grandpa, who made the first successful rice crop on the Ashley River," he said, and Fiona heard a note of pride in his voice. But then he added, "Not that nobody would ever give him credit for it, of course. He was just a nigger from a place nobody around here ever heard of."

Chapter Twenty-One

Just before noon, the wagon rolled into the bustling streets of Charlestown. During the course of their journey, Fiona had learned that Locksley's family was prized for their knowledge of rice cultivation, which she found was the major cash crop for the area. The plantation owner who eventually came into possession of his grandfather, and later his father, grew wealthy on the fruits of their labor. When Locksley was born, his father took him to the owner and struck a deal that when he turned eighteen, his status as slave would change to indenture, and after ten years, he would become a free man.

It was during his indenture that Major Stainton offered a substantial amount to purchase his papers, needing him to start up his new plantation, Edgewater. When the indenture expired, he hired Locksley as his overseer, and Locksley agreed. "I've never known anything else," he told her. "Where would I go? What would I do? He pays good money, and I have free run of the operations. Long as everybody abides by his law, we do fine."

Fiona wondered what "his law" entailed but didn't ask.

They stopped beneath the shade of a large tree with huge, dark green leaves. Scattered on the ground beneath were the remains of its earlier blossoms, some of the biggest flowers she'd ever seen. "Magnolia," Locksley told her. "Smells real sweet in springtime."

Locksley escorted Fiona into the small shop of the dressmaker, introduced her, handed the list of required items to the seamstress, and left. "I don't know how long I will be," he told Fiona. "Don't leave the shop until I return."

Miss Upton was a middle-aged woman with graying blond hair and thick glasses. She fussed over Fiona in quite a motherly way, and Fiona instantly took a liking to her. "So ye've come t' be Mrs. Stainton's lady's maid, have ye?" she asked, revealing her Scottish origins in her speech. "That poor little woman. Used to come in here often when they lived in town. She didna want t' move out to that big old plantation. A farm, that's what she called it. Never did like it."

Fiona sensed Miss Upton thrived on gossip, so she was careful in her reply. "I've only just arrived there, came in yesterday, so I haven't had much time to get to know her."

"From Ireland, are ye? I can tell by th' way you talk. Not many Irish here in Charlestown, but lots down the coast in Savannah, I hear. Now let's see," she said, taking the list and adjusting her spectacles. "What is it her ladyship wants ye t' be wearin' in her service?"

Beatrice Stainton had asked Miss Upton to make two garments appropriate for the station of lady's maid, but "not too exquisite." Miss Upton snickered at this last note. "She wants you to look fine, but not too fine," she laughed. "Probably wants t' keep you out of th' wanderin' eye of that philanderin' husband of hers." She broke off abruptly and looked up at Fiona in alarm. "Oh, dear, I shouldna ha' said that. Please don't repeat it."

Fiona grinned. "Wouldn't dare, but just to let you know, she's already warned me against him." With that, the two got on about their measurements.

Miss Upton was to make two skirts and two white cotton blouses, three aprons and two bonnets, the latter of which required much discussion of how to cover Fiona's unruly crown of thick, red hair. She had also ordered shifts and underclothing. "The stockings and shoes'll have t' come from th' general store. I haven't them here in my shop."

Locksley appeared less than two hours later, and Fiona bade farewell to Miss Upton. "Them dresses'll be ready by end of week," she said to Locksley. "Want me to fetch the stockings and shoes fer ye?" Locksley agreed, Miss Upton took a quick measurement of Fiona's foot, and then they departed.

On the way to the marketplace, Fiona spied the small group of Indians she'd seen yesterday, squatting in the shade of a tree on a square. The trader, McNeill, was nowhere around. Where did they live, she wondered? Where were those high mountains McNeill had spoken about? So much was new and foreign here.

The marketplace was busy in the hot afternoon, and Fiona found it exciting. She'd been to the market in Liverpool, but there had been nothing like this in her experience in Ireland.

There were fruits and vegetables, flowers, chickens, even a couple of live goats, intricate woven baskets, some kind of rough-hulled nut, and gourds, but she saw nothing resembling herbs or spices.

Locksley made his way easily through the throng, recognized by most everyone and greeted warmly. He purchased some of the nuts and a handful of beautiful pink flowers on long stems. Fiona wandered, eyes feasting on the sights and searching for a vendor who might have the chamomile she'd come for. She spotted an old black woman in one far corner whose dark eyes penetrated her gaze, and Fiona was drawn as with an invisible cord to her table.

"Hello," she said hesitantly, unsure of how to address these people. The woman bowed her turbaned head in a serene greeting.

"I been waitin' for you to come to me," she said in a low voice. "Seen you come into th' market, and I knew you'd be wantin' what I have."

Fiona was astounded. "How did you know that? And what do you have that I want?"

The woman smiled. "I knows another wise woman when I sees her." She swept her arm like a wand across the items displayed on her table. "You know herbs and potions," she said. "You came for them herbs."

A shiver crawled up Fiona's spine. Other than her Granny and her Ma, she'd never met anyone with the Sight, but it came to her clearly that this woman was much like them. "I see," she said, recovering from her surprise. "Yes, I did come for a specific herb. Have you any chamomile?"

The woman shuffled among the dried leaves and flowers that were her wares, then produced a handful of dried flowers with faded yellow blossoms. "This what you lookin' for?"

Fiona recognized them instantly. "Yes!" She was pleased to find what she believed would help Lady Beatrice, but then she remembered, she had no money. She looked around and found Locksley standing nearby, watching her. "Please, do you have money? These are the makings for the tea I think will help Lady Beatrice."

Locksley gave her an impassive look, then dealt directly with the old woman, paying her price and waiting for her to put the herb in a small cloth bag which he handed to Fiona. "We must go now," he said. Fiona thanked the old woman and made note of her place in the market. She would visit her again, and both of them knew it.

This time Locksley helped her into the wagon. He hitched up the mare and turned the wagon onto the path homeward. "Be careful of that old hag," he said abruptly after they'd been on the road for a few minutes. "Folks say she's a witch."

"A witch? Why do they say that?" she asked, but she already knew the answer. That old woman had the Sight, the power, and the understanding of the natural and supernatural worlds, and was one of those who could bring the two together, just like her Granny. It frightened many folk.

"Her potions are well-known. She's a hoodoo woman, a Gullah come up from D'fuske. Everybody knows that place is hainted, and some say when that hag puts the curse on you, you're as good as dead."

"She seemed harmless enough to me," Fiona ventured. "And she has a lot of herbs that I recognized, things my Granny taught me to use to heal up sick folk."

He gave her a sideways glance. "Stay away from her," he warned. "And don't tell Miss Beatrice where you got them herbs. She wouldn't drink that tea if she knew."

They arrived at Stainton Hall, as the house was called, in late afternoon. Locksley pulled the wagon to the rear of the house, and Fiona jumped out. As she did, she noticed a large crate of some kind covered with canvas in the back. "What's that?" she asked, curious.

"Nothing you need t' know about. Now go on." Then he said, "Wait!" and he picked up the pink flowers. "These are for the lady. She always likes it when I bring flowers from town." He handed the bundle down to Fiona, flicked the reins, and headed toward the nearby stone building.

Fiona hurried in to find Lady Stainton in her drawing room, doing needle work. "So, did Miss Upton get you fixed up?" she asked abruptly without any greeting.

Fiona curtseyed. "Yes, m'lady. She says the things will be ready by the end of this week. These are for you," she said, handing her the flowers.

"From Locksley?"

"Yes, m'am. He said you like to have fresh flowers from town."

Lady Stainton got a faraway look in her eye, but it vanished almost instantly. "Yes," she said curtly. "He is good about remembering that." She placed them on a nearby table and resumed her stitching.

Fiona held up the pouch with the tea makings. "And look! I found it. The chamomile. If you like, I shall make you a cup before you go to bed, and we can see if it eases your sleeping problems."

Beatrice raised an eyebrow. "Where did you find it?"

"Uh, in the market," Fiona replied, recalling Locksley's warning not to say more.

"Very well. Let me see," Beatrice said, laying aside her needlework.

Fiona took the pouch to her and poured a few of the dried flowers into the palm of Beatrice's little hand. "See that golden blossom?" she said, fingering one of the dried blooms. "That's where nature holds the secret to good sleep."

Beatrice looked up at her and wrinkled her nose. "Looks like a bunch of weeds to me."

Fiona laughed. "I suppose some might call them weeds," she said, "but some of those weeds are very helpful to us." She scrunched a blossom and let the seeds fall into her hand. "If you like, we can plant these in your garden and grow your very own chamomile. That is," she added with caution, "if it seems to work for you."

That night, Fiona brewed a cup of chamomile tea, sweetened it with honey, and Beatrice Stainton slept long and peacefully. The following day, she introduced Fiona to her garden. "Yes," she said. "I think we should plant those weeds here."

Chapter Twenty-Two

The next day, after putting Lady Stainton down for her afternoon nap, Fiona wandered into the garden. It was lovely, designed as she imagined an English garden would be laid out, with gravel paths and neatly pruned shrubs lining the walks. At one end the rose arbor supported late bloomers of pink and white buds on stems carefully trained to intertwine with the latticework. She sat for a moment on a bench and regarded the big house from this vantage point.

The garden was to one side of the building, overlooked by Lady Stainton's windows and the chimney that served the fireplace in her chamber. Several windows lined the second story, and Fiona wondered if Major Stainton's quarters were there. It occurred to her that she hadn't seen him in the house since they'd arrived.

She left the garden and made her way past the front of the house to the other side, where the one-story stone building hunkered beneath the overarching limbs of one of those huge gnarly trees. Major Stainton's office? Or maybe his quarters?

Moving on toward the back of the big house, she saw the major and Locksley unloading the crate they'd brought from Charlestown yesterday. It was obviously quite heavy, so they placed it on the ground and opened it before moving it further.

"Major, I got a bad feeling about this," she heard Locksley say. "Them Injuns not going to like finding some of them missing."

The major retrieved a long-barreled gun from the wooden box. "Just a couple from each crate, those redskins will never know the difference. I'll teach them to threaten me!"

Fiona watched as they took the guns into a wooden barnlike building, then hauled another box clearly marked "Ammunition" into the building. She dashed back to the front of Stainton Hall and into the house, breathing heavily. She hoped to God they hadn't seen her!

So that was the errand the major had sent Locksley on yesterday. He must have gone back to that warehouse and taken some guns from each crate and the box of ammunition. She wondered why the trader and his Indians hadn't removed everything right after the altercation, but she'd seen they were still in town, so perhaps the trader McNeill still had other business in Charlestown.

Fiona returned to her room and took out the small book in which she'd recorded parts of this journey. Carefully, she described the events of the past two days, including her opinion of Major Stainton, which was not flattering, a description of the Indians, and a sketch of Locksley. She was interrupted by the clanging of a loud bell and hurriedly jumped to her feet, stashed the book in its drawer, and entered Lady Stainton's chamber.

"You rang, m'lady?"

Beatrice was sitting on the side of her bed, short legs dangling. "Yes, what did you think that was? A fire bell?"

Fiona stifled a grin. "No, m'lady. What can I do for you?"

She helped Beatrice to the floor, removed the duster in which she had napped, and replaced it with her day dress. When they were finished, Beatrice beckoned Fiona to follow her into the drawing room. "Can you read?" she asked.

Fiona was startled. "Yes, m'lady."

"I would like you to read to me then." Beatrice indicated shelves along one wall that held a number of books. "I brought these from England," she said, "but have not read a one."

"Which would you like me to read?" Fiona asked, going to the shelves and running a finger across the spines, noting they were dusty.

"Pick one. Any one." Beatrice sighed. "I have a lot of catching up to do."

Fiona was curious, and before she knew it, an awkward question came out of her mouth. "Why haven't you read them yourself?"

Beatrice plopped into an overstuffed chair. "Why, indeed! Not that it's any of your business, Fiona, but..." She paused, and Fiona thought she saw the woman's chin quiver. She waited for Beatrice to continue.

"My father," she said with almost a hiss, "deemed it unnecessary to waste money educating me. And so, my dear, I never learned to read." She sighed. "Isn't it odd—the Irish maid can read, but the English lady cannot."

Fiona found no appropriate reply to this, so instead studied the titles. There were works by authors she'd never heard of—Jonathan Swift, Voltaire, John Locke—and then, one she knew, William Shakespeare. She selected it. "Would you like me to read a play by Shakespeare?"

Lady Stainton laid her head back against the chair and closed her eyes. "I must get over my embarrassment," she murmured. "Yes, indeed. Please read me something by that good man."

That night before going to bed, Fiona blew out her lantern and sat looking out of the window, across the rice fields to the river, thinking that her Da had been right after all. This was a better life for her, despite the oddities of this household. She felt sympathy for her mistress and wanted very much to ease her obvious loneliness. She wished Lady Stainton would allow her to visit the slave village, to see Alicia again, and yes, to somehow join in the music and dancing she'd heard that first night.

Which brought her thoughts to her fiddle, tucked securely away in the satchel beneath her bed. She knelt and drew it out, touching it lovingly, thinking of her Da. She sat on the bed in the darkness and ran her fingers across the smooth if dented wood and plucked at the strings as Alicia had done. Quietly. She picked up the bow and ran it silently across the strings, and her fingers ached to play the instrument. Beatrice had forbidden her kind of music, but she must find a way. It was part of her soul.

***

Later that night, Fiona was awakened by shouts: "Fire!" She ran to her window and saw men running toward the barn where the major and Locksley had stashed the guns. The building was engulfed in flames. She quickly donned her dress and tiptoed into Lady Stainton's room.

The chamomile was working—the lady was sound asleep, snoring lightly.

Fiona closed the door between their rooms, pulled on a shawl, and ran out the back door. She stared in horror at the blaze but was glad to see the fire wasn't spreading. The houses in the slave village were all of wood and would burn easily.

A number of slaves had formed a que leading to the river, and those strong-backed workers were passing buckets of water up the hill to the flames. She saw Eliza furiously pumping water from their well, and she ran to help. At first the woman backed away in fear, but Fiona shouted, "Keep pumping! I'll fetch another bucket."

When Eliza's vessel was filled, Fiona replaced it with a second bucket, then ran with the sloshing water across the lawn and down to the fire. Locksley spotted her and ran to take the bucket. "You shouldn't be here, Miss Fiona. It's...it's not your place. And," he added, "it's too dangerous."

"If I'm to live at Edgewater, then I would say it's my place to help protect it. Now, use that water and give me the bucket back. I'll come back with a refill."

Locksley gave her an astounded look, but he did as he was told. When she grabbed the empty bucket and turned to run back to the pump, she ran squarely into the stout figure of Major Stainton.

"What the bloody hell?" he yelled. "What are you doing out here? Where is Beatrice?"

"Sleeping, sir," Fiona replied, rather breathless. "Now, please excuse me. I have water to fetch." She dodged his arm as he reached out to stop her and dashed back to Eliza. She figured there might be bloody hell indeed to pay for that insubordination, but it seemed to her that dousing the fire took precedence.

She was correct in her assumption. The following morning, she found the major in Beatrice's room, reaming her out for allowing her new girl to run wild in the night. "Please, sir, it wasn't Beatrice's doing," Fiona said. "She was sound asleep. I...I took it upon myself to do what I could to help put out the fire."

By this time, Beatrice was up and sitting at the side of the bed. "Fiona, put that stool here, please." Fiona fetched a step stool that Beatrice used to help her out of the high bed, and she stood on it, bringing her eyes level with the major's. "Now," she said harshly to her husband, "you get out of my chambers this minute, and don't you dare tell me what I can and cannot do with my own lady's maid."

"You forget yourself, Lady Stainton," he sneered, emphasizing her name to remind her that she was his wife, not his master. "You would be interested to know that Fiona was fraternizing with a nigger."

Lady Stainton's face fell. "What?" She turned to Fiona. "What is he talking about?"

Fiona's heart was pounding in fear. "I wasn't 'fraternizing,' m'lady. I was toting water buckets that Eliza had filled. I thought," she added, fastening a glare on the major, "to be of help, although from the looks of it this morning, that barn burnt to the ground."

The look the major returned her turned her blood to ice. "You insolent bitch!" he said and stepped forward as if to slap her, but Lady Stainton grabbed his arm before he could deliver the blow.

"Stop it, Nigel. Stop it right now. As you said, she is my girl, and I will deal with this. Now leave!"

Major Stainton gave his wife a foul look, then brought his hand to his waist and stroked the gold watch that seemed to be with him always. He held it up to Fiona, who was now frightened out of her mind. "In time, if you don't behave as a proper lady's maid to this very high-born English lady, I shall see you have some lessons."

At that moment, there was a commotion in the center hallway, and the major jerked the door open. "What? What is it, Locksley?" he said curtly.

Fiona peered out the door to see two black men and Locksley, all of them covered with grime and soot. Locksley held out a long stick with a sharp stone point on one end and three black feathers on the other. "It's this, Major," Locksley said. "This was in the tree next to the barn."

Major Stainton grabbed the spear and examined it. "Well, I'll be damned," he muttered. "Those stinking redskins set that fire."

Locksley and the slaves stood in silence as the major's fury became almost palpable. "I'll bet they got the guns and ammo, too. That's why the place didn't blow up." He glared at Locksley, but neither said anything further.

Lady Stainton had come up behind Fiona and was staring in horror at the weapon. Fiona turned and slipped her arm around the tiny woman and led her away from the scene, quietly shutting the door behind them.

"I...I think I'm going to faint," Beatrice said, and Fiona helped her back into the huge bed. Lying there among the covers and pillows, she looked like a fragile doll.

"May I get Eliza to bring your breakfast?" Fiona asked.

Lady Stainton looked perplexed, then frowned. "No. She's a terrible cook, and she had no business entertaining you last night. She knows, they all know, I simply will not abide the niggers having doings with whites."

"Please, m'lady, it wasn't Eliza's fault. In truth, she shooed me away, but I didn't listen to her."

"Humph."

Fiona remained silent to let Beatrice sort this out in her mind. Surely, she would see the reason in this. And she had no way of knowing what Fiona was certain of, that behind this false accusation was her husband's attempt to punish her for avoiding him at the scene of the fire.

Beatrice looked at Fiona. "Go fetch her, that Eliza, and send her back to the fields. And you, for now, didn't you say you cooked on that ship?"

"Yes'm."

"Then you shall bring me my breakfast this morning. It will serve you right for disobeying my rules."

"But..."

"Hush. I will let it go this time because you are new here. But in the future, you are under no circumstances to have congress with the niggers."

"Does that include Locksley, m'lady?" Fiona knew she was bordering on being insolent, but she needed to know her boundaries.

Beatrice huffed again. "No. You may speak with Locksley. He's... he's a 'necessary.'"

"But isn't he also...uh...a nigger?" She hated the way that word sounded, but it's what her mistress used.

"Why, no, Fiona. He's not. He's different from them. He's not an African. He comes from different blood."

Chapter Twenty-Three

From the moment Beatrice tasted Fiona's scones, which she'd learned to bake at the inn in Liverpool, she'd decided her lady's maid could handle more duties. "Eliza's biscuits were like rocks," she'd said as she savored the light, buttery scones Fiona brought her that first morning. "I want you to be in charge of the kitchen from now on," she raised an eyebrow, and added, "if that is, you think you can handle that."

The plantation had its own farmyard, with several milk cows, many chickens, hogs, an orchard, and a large vegetable garden. Fiona welcomed the chance to return to cooking, but she wasn't sure if indeed she could handle both and do either one justice. "I...I'd like to try, m'lady, but I would need help." Maybe she could train Eliza, but she knew that woman had little talent for or interest in cooking. An idea crossed her mind. "I fed more than thirty hungry sailors three meals a day on that ship, but I had two others in the kitchen helping me."

Beatrice considered this a moment. "But who would help you? We have no white hands on this farm. Only niggers. I don't know if Stainton would pay for any more help."

Fiona knew how it could work, and she inhaled deeply before setting forth her proposal. "There was a girl on the ship, m'lady. Her name is Alicia, and the major bought her and her mother for Edgewater the day he acquired my indenture. I taught her many tricks in the galley, and she became a valuable hand to me. Perhaps she could be brought in to help."

"But she's a nigger girl."

"Yes, m'lady. She's African. Came on board with the rest of the... uh... human cargo." Somehow, she couldn't manage the word 'slaves.'

But Beatrice shook her head. "No, no, no. It would never do."

Fiona knew how Locksley had provided "personal services" to Beatrice; he was the connection between her and her black servants, the message-bearer, the instructions-giver. Beatrice had called him "a necessary."

"M'lady," she ventured, "perhaps you could make me a...what did you call Locksley, a 'necessary?' It seems you need him to go between your family and the Africans to get your field work and other chores done. Perhaps because I'm...Irish, I'm not truly like the other whites, just as Locksley is not, as you say, like the other niggers. So, if you considered me a 'necessary' like him, I could work with Alicia and your other household help and give him more time to oversee things for the major."

At that she stopped and held her breath. She was not ashamed of being Irish, proud of it in fact, but she knew Beatrice held a prejudice against her because of it. Would it be enough to make her see the value in having a second 'necessary' and a justification for allowing her to interact with the Africans?

Beatrice picked up a teaspoon from the breakfast tray and began tapping it on the arm of the chair. She looked out the window. She squirmed in her chair. She tapped the teaspoon faster. She glanced at Fiona, then looked away. Looked at her again, as if to decide how white she really was. "I'll take it up with the major," she said at last. "In the meantime, do you suppose you could summon enough strength to prepare dinner?"

Her sarcasm wasn't lost on Fiona, but she didn't rise to the bait. "If I may help you with dressing, m'lady, and see you situated as you wish for the rest of the morning, I will be happy to prepare dinner. Will it be just for you, or are there others I need to plan for?"

"Eliza always makes for three—myself, the major, and Locksley. The major rarely takes his meals in this house. Locksley serves him in his office. Look for him at twelve-thirty sharp." Her voice was tight, her words clipped.

After helping with her ablutions and dressing, Fiona left Lady Stainton to her needlework in the drawing room. The large clock in the hall rang ten. Rolling up her sleeves, she adjourned to the kitchen, not expecting the major to agree to her proposal, but determined to make the best of things. And she did. She baked a fresh loaf of bread and a batch of muffins into which she put some bits of fresh pear from Edgewater's small orchard. She sliced wedges from a smoked ham and cooked them with onions in a bit of lard, then added a layer of white potatoes, covered the potatoes with cream and set it to bake. It was an old recipe from home, ham and milky potatoes, but one that most everyone loved.

At twelve-thirty, Locksley appeared and was shocked to find Fiona in the kitchen. "I was being punished for 'fraternizing' with Eliza last night in fetching those water buckets," she explained, frowning. "Now, m'lady fancies me doing all the cooking." She shook her head. "I don't know how this is going to turn out, but for now, please take dinner to the major." She handed him a basket with the food, plates, utensils and napkins.

Fiona served Lady Stainton in the drawing room, and 'm'lady' was almost tearful as she tasted the food. "Oh, my," she said with a sigh. "Lovely." She made short work of the casserole and two slices of the fresh bread as well. When she was finished, she looked thoughtful and said, "I will speak with the major this afternoon. Please ask Locksley to send him at once. Or," she added sourly, "when his majesty can fit in a visit with his wife during his busy schedule."

His majesty the major came hurtling into the kitchen shortly after Fiona had finished cleaning up and was trying to decide what to make for supper, the evening meal. "What's this all about?" he boomed at her.

"M'lady has sent Eliza away, and I'm to do both her work and my own as punishment," she replied as evenly as she could manage.

"Did you make that dinner?"

"I did, sir. Was it to your liking?" Who could tell with this volatile man whether he liked the meal or dashed it against the wall.

He groused a bit about Beatrice's choice of punishment, but in the end, he allowed as how the meal had been fine. "Is this what she wants to see me about?"

"In a fashion. She's in the drawing room, sir." When he left, she turned to Locksley. "Well? Did he like it? Did you?

Locksley grinned widely. "I should say so, Miss Fiona. It was probably the best dinner we've had out here, maybe ever."

Fiona leaned back against a table and let out a long breath. "Thank the good Lord for that," she uttered.

Presently, the two heard loud voices coming from the drawing room. The lord and lady of the house were having it out, and Fiona knew it was because of her. "Does this happen often?" she asked Locksley.

"Not so much. They mostly stay out of each other's way."

The arguing ceased, and Major Stainton stormed out of the room, heading toward the kitchen. He was in a rage. "A necessary, now are you? I paid good money for you to wait on Beatrice. I thought it would make her less disagreeable, but no, now she's even more demanding." He took Fiona painfully by her arm and shook her. "Yes, I can see she's right, you little Irish bitch," he fumed. "You aren't white. She says you consort with niggers, want one of them to serve you here in the kitchen. Well," he thrust his face almost into hers. "So be it. Maybe now she will shut up her complaining. If I hear so much as one more word from her about you, I'll throw you out there with those niggers." He looked at his gold watch. "I haven't got time for this woman business." And with that, he slammed out of the kitchen door.

Locksley looked at her with open curiosity. "What you gone and done, Miss Fiona?"

Fiona grinned, but her knees were weak. "Well, I've pissed him for sure," she said. "But if he liked the dinner as much as you say, perhaps he'll get over it. I think he's in for better eating now." She explained to Locksley what had taken place and asked him to bring Alicia to her whenever he could later that day. He left, shaking his head, muttering something unintelligible.

And then she turned to face the music. With dread, she approached the drawing room. Fiona surmised her mistress was likely in a state of high distress. "Are you all right, m'lady?"

Lady Stainton stood facing the window, her shoulders shaking. Fiona approached and touched her shoulder gently. "M'lady?"

Beatrice turned and to Fiona's astonishment, she was laughing. "That old bully," she snorted. "He didn't like it one bit, that part about you being a 'necessary,' but what he hated worse was that for once, I stood up to him." She wiped her eye with a hanky. "He's going along with it for now," she said, sobering. "But watch out. He's vindictive and doesn't like to be crossed. Better lock your door tonight."

Chapter Twenty-Four

Autumn in South Carolina was a pleasant time, cooler, with light winds and mostly sunny skies, but Locksley seemed uneasy about the upcoming rice harvest. "It's not done until it's done, Miss Fiona," he told her one day when she asked him what was wrong. "There's storms come up this time of year been known to wipe out a whole year's crops."

Fiona knew about those storms. Those hurricanes, they called them. She'd been in that one on board the ship, and it was enough to last her a lifetime. But this year, the weather was fair through October, and the slaves, overseen by Locksley, brought in an abundant crop of beautiful golden rice that Fiona learned how to cook to perfection. She had been allowed to bring Alicia into the kitchen, where she continued to school her on food preparation, and both the major and the lady seemed satisfied at the arrangement.

She avoided Major Stainton if at all possible but enjoyed her time with Beatrice. The two planned an herb garden to be planted among the flower beds in the spring, with parsley, sage, mint, rosemary, thyme, lavender, and bee balm for kitchen use. Fiona had located seeds in the Charlestown market, which she was allowed to visit occasionally in the company of Locksley.

She added chamomile, feverfew, flowering yarrow, wormwood and tansy to use in case of headache and other maladies. She'd also found some spices at the market, cinnamon, nutmeg, and black pepper, but remembering the English preference for bland food, used them and the dried herb seasonings she'd purchased only sparingly.

In early November, Major Stainton surprised her and Beatrice late one morning, bursting unannounced into the drawing room. "I'm going to invite some very important people here to discuss the Indian problem," he told them. "There's talk of troubles with the French in the northern colonies, and they're out to entice our South Carolina Indians to join them." He was so irate Fiona thought he might spit on the floor. She knew nothing of these problems, but she remembered the spear left behind as a calling card the night the Indians took back their guns and ammunition and burned down the barn. She couldn't help but wonder if Stainton's anger wasn't more about that than some far away Indian troubles.

He paced and carried on while Fiona and Lady Stainton looked on in astonishment. Later Fiona learned that he'd never entertained anyone here at the plantation, as if he were ashamed of it—or of his wife's deformity. He'd used Floretta and her house for his business and political dealings. Why now had he decided to entertain at Edgewater? At last he sputtered down a bit and turned to his wife.

"Do you think you can organize a proper feast, Beatrice? Isn't that something the lady of the house is supposed to be in charge of?" His tone was just short of rude.

Beatrice turned pale, then two red spots appeared on her cheeks. "Why, of course, dear husband. It's just that I have never been asked." Her retort was icy.

Fiona stepped in. "I am certain, sir, that m'lady can plan a most elegant dinner party, and I will make every effort to ensure her plans are executed properly."

He turned to her with a sneer. "Make every effort? Is that the best you can do? I don't want just *every effort*! You must be damnably sure you can do this, or..."

"Or what, Nigel?" Lady Stainton interrupted, standing. "Would you prefer to bring your whore here to serve you properly?"

"You, my wife, are out of line."

"It is you, my husband, who is out of line," she replied calmly, giving him an ingratiating smile. "I am pleased to be able to plan and prepare a dinner party for you and your friends. May I ask how many you expect to attend? And do you have any special requests for the menu?"

At her words, the major took a deep breath in an attempt to regain control of his temper, then proceeded to tell the women what he had in mind. He was inviting the Royal Governor himself, James Glen, and members of his Privy Council, but not the Commons. "This is an issue of great importance to the king, and to the royal prerogative, and I see no need to involve any other locals unless and until there is a reason to. Not all, it is whispered, care much for royal prerogative." He turned to go and said over his shoulder, "I shall have Locksley bring you my guest list. I will not be inviting wives, as this business is not to their interest."

After he was gone, Beatrice looked at Fiona with a bemused smile. "He seems to think because I was born small in body that I am also small in mind."

"Nothing could be further from the truth, m'lady," Fiona replied.

"I know that, silly girl. But until now, I have had little opportunity, except in the design of this house, to show that I have a brain and know how to use it."

"If I may dare say so, m'lady, it sounds as if the major thinks little of all female minds. I cannot imagine that wives would not be interested to hear about Indian affairs that might affect them as well as their husbands."

"I do not know any of their wives, as I've never been invited into polite Charlestown society," Beatrice sniffed. "Perhaps they have no brains." And at that she gave a rough laugh, but Fiona heard the bitterness behind it.

The meeting and dinner were scheduled for a date in late November. At first Lady Stainton asked Fiona to write down the menu items, which included traditional foods as would be served in England, roast of beef, Yorkshire pudding, potatoes, peas, and custard pie. Fiona was horrified. "But, m'lady, I've never cooked a roast of beef, only had it as jerky on the ship. Nor have I any idea how to prepare a Yorkshire pudding, although I have heard of it. And I have not seen English peas in the market in town, and I don't believe they're grown here."

She could see Beatrice was dismayed. "I'm told people of...of our stature dine in such a manner," she said. "What am I to do?"

"Perhaps, just for this one affair, the major would consider bringing in a more experienced cook. Someone from Charlestown who knows the proper ways to make such a feast and who perhaps knows where to acquire the ingredients," Fiona suggested.

"No!" Beatrice's reply was sharp and vehement. "I told him I could do this, and I will. You must learn how to prepare these things...and find the damnable peas!"

Fiona thought fast. She could see disaster looming. "Perhaps, m'lady, it would be good to offer something different, something extraordinary that the Governor and their Excellencies do not get at table in Charlestown."

Beatrice looked at her askance. "What are you suggesting?"

Fiona swallowed, gathered her courage, and made it up as she went along. "Why don't you serve a meal of things grown here on the plantation? It could be an example of the wealth and prosperity that has been made from this land. I believe it would make the major look good in the eyes of these men."

Lady Beatrice considered this for a long moment. "And what, exactly, would you put on the table of the Royal Governor?"

Taking a deep breath, Fiona forged on. "We have fine fat hogs here, m'lady. I know how to make hogshead cheese."

At this Beatrice brightened. "I know the city folk are fond of this. Go on."

"We could roast a pig rather than beef. I have done that on many occasions back home." Lady Stainton made a face, but Fiona assured her it was a delicious dish. "We can also serve a roast hen or ducks, maybe some fish from the river, and vegetable puddings to go alongside."

Lady Stainton gave one of her humphs, but then she broke out into a rare smile.

"Brilliant. Simply brilliant. And if the major is not pleased, so be it. He's the one brought me here to this godforsaken outback. He will eat the fruits of that decision."

CHAPTER TWENTY-FIVE

The Royal Governor James Glen and members of his Privy Council, accompanied by a small regiment of horsemen, arrived by coaches around mid-day of the appointed meeting and were greeted by the major, Lady Beatrice, Locksley, Fiona, and a small assemblage of black servants who were dressed in formal serving attire as would be found proper in Britain. Fiona had managed to convince the Staintons that continuing to hold their African workers totally at bay was against their best interests, that they would gain better value from them if assigning the most trusted and reliable to become house servants, under Locksley's keen eye and Fiona's instruction. Among them were Alicia, Eliza, and Alicia's mother, who Fiona had learned was now called Arlevia.

The Governor was a thin-faced man with a rather large nose and full lips who wore the requisite powdered wig of officialdom. A high-collared blouse rose to his chin over his thin neck. He wore a red jacket with elaborate gold fasteners, white breeches, and black shoes with gold buckles. The others were in similar dress, and the major had donned his full military regalia to greet them.

Lady Stainton had selected her most elegant day dress for this greeting, and this evening had instructed Fiona to help her into a sumptuous gown that nearly buried the small woman in its diaphanous layers of azure and lavender. Fiona wished she could advise Beatrice against wearing it, because she looked more like a toy princess doll rather than the wife of a British major. But this was no time to criticize anything about Beatrice. She was aglow with pride at what she had done, and Fiona would do nothing to dampen her spirits.

The party was escorted into the large parlor across from the drawing room, where a light repast and drinks were served, and all was cordial, it seemed, among those gathered. Fiona's curiosity had blazed over the preceding days as to what these elite gentlemen would discuss.

What exactly was "the Indian problem?" She had not seen any

more Indians on her few forays into Charlestown since that first week she'd arrived.

The guests were later shown to their quarters on the second floor of Stainton Hall to refresh themselves, and the major strode off to his office. After settling Beatrice down for her nap, Fiona headed for the kitchen, where the last of the preparations were being made for the feast.

The men reconvened in the parlor at five, where Fiona, now wearing her own best lady's maid attire, first served Regents Punch, a lovely golden brew of tea-infused champagne, rum, and brandy with fruit floating within the crystal serving bowl. Lady Stainton did not wish to be present when the liquor was served.

Fiona lingered as long as she dared, wanting to listen in on the conversation. It was clear that the governor was very well aware of the "Indian problem," although unlike the major, he considered it more of a French and English problem than one with the indigenous natives.

"As you know, gentlemen, we value the trade between ourselves and the Indians," he said to the group. "It is in our best interest to establish and maintain peace with those who dwell on our borders. The French are recruiting Indians in the north country to fight against our English forces and those of the colonial militia in Pennsylvania and Virginia. We must make and maintain friendship with our South Carolina Indians— the Cherokee, Creeks, and Catawbas, who in truth act as a buffer that protects our settlers against any French invasion here in the south."

Fiona made her way out of the room but left the door slightly ajar, hoping to eavesdrop further on this conversation. She dared stay only a minute more, however, perchance of being caught.

"Those redskins can't be trusted," she heard the major say. "One day they're your friend, the next they'll cut your scalp away without a thought."

"Hear, hear!" she heard another man reply. "Indians are all murderers. All they know is war. They fight amongst themselves, tribe against tribe. They have fought against our settlers, slaughtering innocents, including women and children. Why should we want to deal with them? I say kill 'em all." At that, Fiona ducked away and made haste for the kitchen.

She and Locksley, the two 'necessaries,' were the only ones allowed to serve that evening. As the first course was laid out and ready to present, she went to fetch Lady Stainton. Entering her chamber, she could swear the little woman had grown by inches, and she looked almost regal in her gown.

"M'lady, you look lovely," she exclaimed. "You look..."

"Taller?" Beatrice grinned, raised the hem of her skirt, and revealed shoes with platforms a few inches high. "Had them made for my wedding. I refused to look like a dwarf on that day, even though I had no taste for marrying Nigel. I had no choice in that matter, but I did choose to make a good appearance." She paused, then added, "Only trouble is, I cannot walk well even in normal shoes. These are dreadfully more difficult. I must depend on you to help me across into the dining room."

The two made their way out of the lady's chamber at the midsection of the house, crossed the wide hallway, and Fiona opened the grand doorway into the large dining room. The men, who had not yet been seated, looked up, startled. Storm clouds crossed Major Stainton's face, but Lady Stainton remained composed.

"Good evening, gentlemen, and welcome to Edgewater, my home," she said, emphasizing the latter. "I pray you will enjoy your repast tonight, and your stay here as well. I have asked my staff to prepare a very special meal for your delight and enjoyment."

At this the assembled group murmured their approval. The lady continued. "It will not be the usual fare as is found normally on occasions of such importance as this in Charlestown," she said, raising her chin slightly. "Everything you will be served was grown, raised, or hunted on this plantation and prepared by plantation staff." She turned and smiled sweetly at her husband, but the smile did not reach her eyes. "We are proud of what the major has accomplished here and wish to share it with your Excellencies." She returned her gaze to the others. "And now, gentlemen, if you will excuse me, I will take my leave. I understand that the conversation here is not for frail, feminine ears. Please, enjoy your evening."

With that, she took Fiona's arm and allowed her to lead her back into the hallway and close the door behind them. Fiona was astounded.

"Lady Beatrice, why aren't you joining the dinner party?"

Beatrice clenched her fingers around Fiona's arm. "He made it clear by not inviting the wives that women weren't welcome at the table. At any rate, I couldn't stand to sit there in his company and hear him rant on about the Indians," she said. "And besides, these shoes hurt like the devil. Please return me to my room, help me out of this ridiculous dress and shoes, but hurry, I'm sure the Excellencies are impatient to see what plunder we've made here at Edgewater."

Fiona did as her mistress bade, and as she returned to the kitchen and the dinner party at hand, a small part of her heart swelled at Beatrice's courage and fortitude. She prepared a tray for Beatrice and hurried to deliver it before starting the meal in the dining room.

The meal was served in several courses—crab soup, succulent and smoky flavored pig that was roasted over an open pit, yams cooked in whisky, and more dishes prepared from that which was grown on the plantation—and each seemed to deepen the dark look on Major Stainton's face. He was obviously embarrassed by having his elite guests served what he considered peasant food. But in the end, his guests raved about the meal and praised Lady Stainton's choice for the evening's banquet.

"Well done, Major," the Governor said as they rose to retire to the parlor for brandy. "I haven't had that fine a meal since I left Scotland."

"Hear, hear," the others joined in, and Fiona, listening behind the servants' door, smiled. The major had been outfoxed in his own den. He would hate her for it, but he had not lost esteem in the eyes of these important men, so she doubted he would berate her unduly. Besides, it had been his wife's plan, hadn't it?

CHAPTER TWENTY-SIX

Fiona later learned from Locksley, who was asked to serve the gentlemen in the parlor and remain to meet any of their needs over the course of the evening, that Governor Glen had been petitioned by the Cherokee a few years before to build a fort on the western frontier, not only to protect trade between their tribe and the English, but also to protect them from their ancient enemies, the Creeks.

Some of the men on the Privy Council agreed, but others were of the same mind as the major, that the only way to resolve the Indian problem was to rid the country of them altogether. To prove his point that the Indian problem was more immediate, Major Stainton escorted the entire entourage to the scene of the fire and showed them the spear that had identified the perpetrators of the crime.

"Did he mention that he entered into trade with these same Indians?" Fiona wanted to know, but she did not let on that she knew how Stainton had tried to cheat the Indians.

Locksley smiled sardonically. "What do you think?"

Both knew the major spoke only what he saw to be to his advantage.

Locksley had learned, however, that the Governor was moving ahead to build that fort, to be called Fort Prince George after the present Prince of Wales, George III, and was planning a journey himself to the site to placate the Indians he felt should be kept in alliance with the British.

The carriages departed the following morning after a late breakfast, and only when they had turned out of the lane onto the rough dirt road back toward Charlestown did Major Stainton unleash his ire. He slammed into the drawing room where Fiona was reading to Lady Stainton.

"What the hell were you thinking, woman? Serving pig and yams to the Royal Governor? Nigger food!"

Beatrice retained her composure. "I heard, sir, that they were very pleased with the meal, and I thought, possibly mistakenly so, that I was honoring you and your accomplishments here on the farm."

"Farm! This is not a farm! This is a plantation, and it is huge. It is great! Very, very great!"

"My point exactly, husband. What we produce here is exported and sold to your financial advantage. You, unlike those others, do not depend on ships bringing English fare to your table. You provide for yourself. And your family, too, of course."

Nigel Stainton stared at his wife in disbelief that she would dare defy him, but he was at a loss as to how to reply to such compliments. So instead, he turned to Fiona. "You! It was your doing, wasn't it?"

Fiona stood up out of both deference and defiance. "I beg pardon, sir," she said innocently. "I...I took my orders from m'lady." She saw Stainton's jaw tighten, and she dared not say more.

"I warned you the day I bought you that I would abide no insubordinance," he growled.

At that, Fiona couldn't keep her tongue. "Pardon sir, but you did not buy me. You bought my indenture for my service to your wife. Service which I performed last evening at her bidding."

"Leave her alone, Nigel!" Beatrice piped up. "She's correct. The whole thing was my idea. The preparation, which I believed was highly satisfactory, was all that was under Fiona's care. Now get out of my sight. You make me sick."

Fiona's eyes widened. She wanted to disappear into the shadows of the room, but there was no escape. She watched as the major approached his wife. He raised his hand as if to slap her, but she glared at him defiantly.

"Must I remind you of the legal papers you signed when you agreed to marry me, Nigel? The clause there that says if I am in any way harmed, or returned to England, that you will forfeit all that came as my dowry, including this plantation?" She stood and barely reached his chest in height, but her tiny body belied an inner strength, and to Fiona's mind, a rage surfaced that had been boiling for many years. "Now leave! Go to your precious office and don't darken my house again."

"Your house! This is not your house! I built this house. I built this plantation. I have made you a lady when you would have been a cripple and an embarrassment to your family."

"You have made me nothing, Nigel, except a prisoner in this hot hellhole. Now leave."

Fiona wasn't breathing by this time, wondering what the arrogant major would do to his tiny wife. She almost feared for Beatrice's life. But the man wheeled and left the room, slamming the door behind him.

Beatrice collapsed into her chair and began to cry. "I hate him so, Fiona. And I'm afraid of him."

Fiona didn't know what to say, so she said what everyone seemed to think solved every problem. "Can I make you tea, m'lady?"

** * **

That evening as Fiona was finishing up her duty in the kitchen, Locksley appeared at the door. He looked apprehensive. "Major Stainton wishes a word with you, Miss Fiona."

Here it comes, she thought. She was in for an upbraiding, she was sure, probably loud and abusive. But would he beat her? Images of the lashings on the *Lady Caroline* came to mind. Surely, he wouldn't do something so obvious that Lady Beatrice would notice. She dried her hands, removed her outer apron, adjusted her cap to cover her wanton curls, and said, "Very well, then."

She followed Locksley to the major's office, which by now she knew was also his personal quarters. Locksley knocked, and the major shouted, "Come in." Locksley opened the door for Fiona and gave her what could only be a sad and apologetic look, and then he left.

"You wished to see me, sir?" Fiona managed, her voice a bit squeaky and her knees trembling.

The major had been standing by his large desk, staring into the fire that burned in the hearth. He turned to Fiona, and she saw that he held a crystal glass filled with amber liquid. A nearly empty decanter sat on the desk. The major's face was florid, and Fiona surmised he'd been nursing his anger throughout the day, and he was about to take it out on her. She was glad Lady Stainton had already gone to bed for the night.

He reached for his gold watch, unfastened it from his waistcoat, and laid it aside on the desktop. "You little bitch," he growled. "You little Irish bitch." He took two steps toward her, and instinctively she took two backwards. He reached for her and grabbed her painfully by the arm. "You disgraced me in front of the governor and councilmen, and now you will pay for it."

Before Fiona could reply, the major swung her around and slammed her face into the desk. He held her roughly while he unfastened his breeches. He shoved his hand beneath her dress and wrenched away her knickers. It happened so quickly and unexpectedly, Fiona had no time to cry out, but she did so as he painfully inserted himself into her. "Sir, please, no!" she managed, but he was on her with a vengeance.

She knew what was happening. She'd seen horses and dogs used in the same manner when mating. Her world began to spin, and suddenly it turned dark. She regained her senses moments later, when the major had finished and pulled away. She could not move and continued to lay still, face down, her upper body support by the desk, her legs dangling over the side. All she could see was that big gold watch lying on the desk right by her nose.

"Get up, bitch," Stainton demanded, taking her forcefully by the arm again and yanking her to her feet. "Get up and get out of my sight. And if you ever cross me again, you will know what punishment awaits you." He paused, buttoning his breeches and reattaching his gold watch. "And if you give so much as a hint of this to Lady Stainton, I will see that you come to a serious accident, one that you will not survive."

Stunned and shaken beyond all imagination, Fiona managed to pull up her knickers and flee. Locksley was nowhere in sight. She ran down to the river and immersed herself in the water, wanting to wash away what had just happened. Wanting to believe it was a nightmare and that she would wake up.

Knowing that it had all been too real.

Eventually she gathered herself enough to wade out of the water and make her way back to the house. In her room, she took off her soiled clothing and donned the comfort of her nightgown. She crawled into bed and reached for the amulet that lay beneath her pillow. "Why, Granny, why?" she sobbed silently. She knew she had been a good and true servant to Lady Stainton, and that although she had instigated the choice of food for the feast, it had been gratifying to see her mistress happy for a change as she took charge of the planning.

All this for lack of English peas, she thought, disgusted. And then another thought alarmed her. Could she be with child? She had no idea how long it took to find out, but she knew for sure it was now a possibility. That's how children were made. What would she do if it were so? Fear turned her skin cold. What would happen to her? She wouldn't be able to hide it from Lady Stainton. Would the major carry out his threat of an "accident?" She had no doubt he was capable of murder.

Quickly she took out Granny's book of spells and thumbed through it by candlelight.

There were many receipts in here for the use of herbs for medicinal purposes. Was there one to prevent conception?

The next morning, Fiona brewed herself a special tea while preparing Lady Stainton's breakfast tray, an infusion of dried parsley she'd acquired from the market and chamomile. She would drink it many times throughout the day, hoping that what she'd read in Granny's book was an effective potion.

Three days later, her blood flowed. Tears of relief streamed down her cheeks. She wasn't sure whether it was her natural cycle, or if the tea had worked its magic. Either way, she didn't care.

All she cared about was avoiding that evil man at all costs.

Chapter Twenty-Seven

Scarcely a week after the dinner party, a messenger arrived at Edgewater with a letter to Lady Stainton from the wife of one of the members of the Privy Council. Beatrice opened the letter, then handed it to Fiona to read:

"My dear Lady Stainton, Would You do Us the Pleasure of Coming for Tea Tuesday Next?" she read, then glanced up at Beatrice. She saw the astonishment on her mistress's face before her features flushed with pleasure.

"Go on," Beatrice urged anxiously.

Fiona read the time and address of the hostess, and her request for a reply by the messenger who had arrived with this note. At the bottom of the paper was a postscript: "If you would be so kind as to share the receipts for that wonderful meal my husband so enjoyed at Edgewater, we would receive them with deepest gratitude."

"Oh, my," Beatrice squeaked. "Oh, my, oh, my!" She did a little hop right in front of Fiona, then looked abashed and calmed herself.

"The messenger is in the kitchen taking tea," Fiona said. "Would you like me to write a reply for him to take upon his return?"

Beatrice gave Fiona a radiant smile. "I would be ever so grateful," she said. "And perhaps soon it would be a good idea for you to teach me how to read and write."

Fiona wrote down Lady Stainton's reply on some creamy white stationery that was in a box in the drawing room. It had never been opened, for obvious reasons. When the messenger was ready to depart, in an unusual move Beatrice waved at him from the front steps. Then she turned to Fiona. "I can't wait to tell that bastard Nigel that Lady Atkin has requested the receipts for the meal he so distained."

Fiona's stomach lurched, then tightened into a hard knot. "Please, m'lady. Do not tell him. It will likely just reignite his anger that he wasn't consulted on the meal."

Beatrice frowned. "Well, if you think so. He's such a difficult man."

Fiona grimaced. *If you only knew, m'lady.*

After promising to write down the ingredients and directions for preparing the dishes that had been served, Fiona excused herself to attend to directing Alicia in cooking the evening meal. Later, before retiring, she brought the box of stationery into her room and began trying to remember what she'd done to cook, season and serve each dish. She herself had had no receipts to go by, so she'd made them up from her experience and imagination. Oh, lord, help me, she thought as she began her chore.

The following week, she attended Lady Stainton as her well-dressed lady's maid, and was happy to see the little woman, once ignored by Charlestown's society, welcomed into their company. It occurred to her fleetingly that perhaps Beatrice hadn't been purposely ignored, that she was just never introduced to these elite ladies by her odious husband who so distained his wife's deformities.

* * *

Fiona turned fifteen on the night of the winter solstice, the darkest night of the year and a holy one to those who honored the old ways. She let only Alicia know that it was her birthday, and after the evening meal was over and put away, and Lady Stainton in bed, Fiona drew her Da's fiddle from its hiding place beneath her bed and crept down to the slave village.

She knew where Alicia and her family lived and, keeping to the shadows of the large fire that lit up the night in the center of the slave quarters, she made her way and knocked tentatively at the door.

Alicia's eyes widened in surprise and fear when she saw Fiona, then she spied the fiddle. A wide smile crossed her face. "In," she beckoned in a hushed voice and quickly shut the door behind her. Alicia's English was still halting, but she had learned much in the months she'd been at Edgewater, a lot of it from Fiona in the kitchen.

Alicia's mother, Arlevia, came into the room, her little boy on one hip. She looked at Alicia with a deep frown, but her daughter shook her finger and told her not to worry. She showed Fiona to a rough-hewn chair and brought a tin cup of water as refreshment. Fiona smiled. If only everyone was as kind as this young girl.

Without another word, Fiona picked up her fiddle, sounded it for tuning and made adjustments. When she drew her bow across the strings, it was as if a lost life force began to flow through her. She closed her eyes and let the old familiar music fill the small cabin. It was a slow tune that issued forth at first, a bit melancholy but one her mother had loved. She didn't notice at first, but Alicia went to her small bed and reached beneath it. She returned with an instrument made from a hollowed-out gourd, with a long neck and four strings stretched across it. Fiona recalled seeing something like it the night she'd first gone down to the slave village. "*Ngoni,*" Alicia said.

She took a stool across from Fiona, held the instrument sideways as she had done with the fiddle on the ship, and began plucking the instrument. She sang a lively tune in her native language, and Fiona was spellbound. She listened for a few moments, then picked up her fiddle and hit a stride in tune with Alicia's music. The two played happily for half an hour, each challenging the other to stretch the voices of their distinctive but similar instruments to create a sound unlike anything Fiona had ever known.

Fiona dared not linger too long lest her mistress awoke and called her, but as she bade farewell and crept back out into the night, she felt a joy in her heart and a lightness in her step that kept the rest of the shadows in her life at bay, at least for this, her birthday night.

* * *

Lady Stainton chose to avoid any celebration of Christmas other than to go into Charlestown to services at the Anglican Church. She and Nigel had received an invitation that he could not turn down—the governor himself had invited them to dine with him and his wife after services.

Beatrice was nervous as a new bride as Fiona helped her into her finest holiday dress, never worn on this side of the Atlantic all the years she'd been in America. She allowed Fiona to dress her hair in a less severe style, and she donned a jaunty hat.

Since she was going in company with the major, and they planned to stay over in Charlestown, Beatrice gave Fiona the day off and waved gaily to her from the window of the carriage as they departed. "Merry Christmas!" Fiona had never seen her so happy.

CHAPTER TWENTY-EIGHT

Since there was no feast to prepare, no mistress to serve, Fiona found herself at loose ends. She was not used to having free time. She first went to Lady Stainton's chamber to straighten it and make it ready to receive her mistress upon her return. She checked the parlor and the drawing room, which were now cleaned daily by Arlevia, who Fiona had recruited as part of the new servant staff at Stainton Hall. Everything in each room was spotless, as was the kitchen.

She wandered into the kitchen garden and looked down the hill toward the shanties that were the slave quarters, and she was surprised to see Locksley leave his own singular quarters behind the kitchen and head toward the rice fields. Did he not get a day off? She supposed not, but as she observed his progress, she saw he wasn't headed to the fields, but instead went directly toward the crude dwellings.

Fiona wandered a little further and took a seat on a low rock wall. As she watched, she saw several black men build and light the fire in the center of the village. Locksley emerged from the shed Fiona knew to be the cookhouse for the slaves carrying a large black pot which was placed on supporting arms then moved across the center of the fire. Steam rose as the contents, which she supposed was water, began to boil.

Arlevia came out with a basket of ears of corn, followed by Alicia with peeled potatoes and yams, which they put into the pot. They returned to the shed and came back with what Fiona recognized as sausage that was made on the plantation. Into the pot it went, and sometime later, they added the strange little white hard-shelled sea creatures they caught with their nets.

As this was going on, the entire slave community emerged from their dwellings and gathered around the fire. They were dressed in what must be their finest clothing, because it wasn't the attire they wore in their field and farm work. It was Christmas for them as well, Fiona realized, knowing that most of them had been converted from their native religions to the white man's faith. Or at least the white man thought so. She remembered how she, too, was a Christian, but she, like her family and most of their friends, had never let go of the Old Ways either.

Fiona couldn't help herself. She was alone, had no one but these people to share her day with. So, she strode down to the edge of the village. She cringed a bit when the slaves, who were enjoying a rare day of celebration, saw her and grew quiet. Locksley turned and was obviously surprised to see her.

"Would it be wrong for me to join you?" she asked him? "I...I am, after all, a necessary like yourself."

At that, Locksley laughed. "Yes, Miss Fiona, if only you don't tell the master and missus. You're pushing your limits."

Still Fiona hesitated. "Ask them," she said to Locksley, indicating the crowd of Africans looking on in curiosity and not a little fear. "I won't come if they're not comfortable with me here."

Locksley asked the gathered crowd for their permission to allow Fiona, the only white face among them, to share their holiday. At first no one said anything. Then Arlevia stepped forward. "This woman save my life," she declared. "And my baby's."

Alicia added, "Saved mine as well. And has brought some of us to serve at the house. I say, let her come."

Then they all seemed to look to Locksley for a final decision. He took a deep breath and declared with resignation, "This is the birthday of our great Lord. Who are we not to allow all of his sheep to celebrate?"

To Fiona, he muttered as she came closer. "Girl, you gonna get yourself in more deep trouble if you not careful."

His warning wasn't lost on her. "I know, Locksley. I have been very careful after...well, you know."

After that, they let it go. The boiled meal was delicious, served up with fresh bread and a yam pie. Afterward, the enslaved people began to sing as they cleaned up their dishes and utensils. Theirs were not the songs of the English Christmas, but songs that they had brought with them from their African homes. As the sun began to set over the Ashley River, Alicia brought out her *ngoni,* and others retrieved similar instruments, along with primitive drums that were nothing more than hollow gourds, and scarves into which dried bones were wrapped that served as rattles. And the merriment began.

Alicia mimed to Fiona to bring out her fiddle, and she didn't have to ask twice. Fiona dashed uphill to her room, grabbed the fiddle and bow, and was back in short order. At first the musicians stopped and watched her apprehensively, but she gave them a confident grin and launched into many of her favorites from back home. Alicia picked up the tunes on her *ngoni*, adding a distinct syncopation to the music. Other musicians joined in, playing their humble, homemade instruments and following the music as best they could. The fast fiddle tunes soon had others under its spell, and they began a circle dance that left them laughing and breathless.

The sun was down when at last Fiona laid the fiddle across her lap and tilted her head back, sweaty and laughing. As she was catching her breath, she was approached by an older man who wore a black wide-brimmed hat with a white band. He indicated he wanted to hold her fiddle. Unsure of what to do, Fiona looked at Locksley.

"It's fine, Miss Fiona, again if you say nothing about this entire evening. This is James, their spiritual leader. He can be trusted."

Hesitantly, she handed her precious fiddle and bow to the man, who upon receiving it gave her a slight bow. Then he placed the instrument beneath his chin and ran the bow hesitantly across the strings. At first, they gave forth an awkward squeal, and James stopped abruptly. He looked at the strings and studied the frets. He placed his fingers on the neck of the instrument and tried again, this time with better effect but not musical.

Fiona stood up and showed him some of the methods of fiddle playing she'd learned from her Da as a child. If she could learn to play it at such a young age, surely this man who showed such keen interest might pick it up as well. James succeeded on a limited basis, then smiled profusely and handed the fiddle back to Fiona.

"Many thanks, Missus Fiona," he said in a deep, resonant voice. He turned to the gathered group whose black skin now glistened in the firelight and began to sing, and everyone else but Fiona joined in, even Locksley. The song was both passionate and mournful, sung in an African language, which Fiona knew was forbidden. She saw some of the women wipe their eyes as they joined in, and the music flowed as slowly and sweetly as the river below them. James led a second number, this one in English, that spoke of crossing the River Jordan into the Promised Land. Into freedom. Their message this Christmas night was clear—they wanted their freedom— a message that made Fiona long for her own freedom as well.

The air grew chill, and Fiona knew it was time for her to take her leave. She thanked them for the meal and the music, then went back to her room. She lit her lantern, changed into her nightdress, and took out her book wherein she had recorded much of this journey. She sketched from memory the happy people dancing in spite of their lot in life. She had not made any notation of the major's attack on her. Maybe, just maybe, if she tried hard enough, she could let it go.

Maybe.

***

The Staintons returned home the following afternoon, and the major had the good grace to help his wife down from the carriage. Seeing Fiona on the front steps, he quickly looked away, and without bidding Beatrice goodbye, turned on his heel and headed for his lair.

Lady Stainton watched him go and let out a heavy sigh. "I thought perhaps this event might have changed him," she said. "But they say you can't change people. He seemed to enjoy the governor's attention and the company of the other guests, but when the meal was served, I watched his face, and I could see the anger return."

"But why?" Fiona asked as they entered the darkened center hallway.

"Because, my dear, Mrs. Atkin and Mrs. Glen collaborated on the menu, and they used your receipts to duplicate what you served here. They had the usual roast beef and Yorkshire pudding, potatoes, all that lot. But alongside they served pork her man had cooked over a pit, just like Locksley did, those delicious yams cooked in whiskey, and that rice dish you made up." She gave a little laugh as they entered her chamber. "Mrs. Atkin said you called it 'rice cream' on the receipt, but she decided it was so good, henceforth it will be called Charlestown ice cream." She laughed again. "I guess that must have really gotten Nigel's goat."

Fiona's stomach was in a knot. It wasn't Nigel's goat she was worried about. Would he come after her with another of his "punishments?

CHAPTER TWENTY-NINE

Winter in the low country was not cold like in Ireland, but the wind coming off the nearby sea could be brisk, and Fiona was glad when March arrived. The camellias were bright spots during the winter, and flowering bushes began their spring show early in March. In April, she and Beatrice planted the herb garden they had planned in the fall, and spring rains graced it bountifully.

Locksley and even the major were busy overseeing the slaves who were preparing the fields in readiness to plant the rice that would sustain them in the year to follow. Fiona had learned that it was rice that created the wealth for the plantation owners, money that also trickled down to the merchants and traders in Charlestown.

Major Nigel Stainton was both plantation owner and trade merchant. She had witnessed his interaction with the fur trader McNeill the first day she arrived, and she suspected that he later had made arrangements with Captain Michael or some other sea captain to take the deerskins and pelts he'd bought from the Indians to England, where they were highly prized. He had his fingers in two pockets, but as for his household, his fists were tight. Beatrice had to request any funds they needed for food, clothing or other supplies, as she had no money of her own. Still, the new household staff had uniforms befitting their station, mainly because Beatrice had begun to entertain, on a very limited basis, her new friends from Charlestown, and she had pointed out to the major that she would not want him to be shamed by having shabbily dressed servants in their house.

Emboldened by her sojourn into the slave village on Christmas day, Fiona found ways to creep out on nights that were warm enough and take her fiddle to Alicia's cabin, where she taught her African friend how to play in return for Alicia's instruction on the *ngoni*. At times they invited James to join them, but they did so at great risk. Even Locksley didn't know of these clandestine meetings.

One day late in April, the major and Beatrice paid a visit to the

British officials in Charlestown. There had been more rumors and tales of horrific Indian attacks on British settlers in the north, and Governor Glen was eager to lay out a plan to protect South Carolina's western borders. In addition, he was acutely aware that the slave population was more than double that of the whites, and having Indian allies would be valuable in suppressing any slave revolt. It was this latter issue that most interested Stainton.

In their absence, Fiona dared to ask Alicia if she thought the black folk would be able to have a little frolic, which is what they called their musical parties, that evening after their work was done. It was agreed upon that they would all meet by the fire after sundown, and Fiona waited eagerly to join in the music and dancing.

The merriment was in full swing when suddenly one of the women let out a scream and pointed into the darkness. Fiona turned to see what was wrong and to her horror, she saw Nigel Stainton emerge into the firelight, his expression furious. Locksley was not far behind him, looking fearful for the first time since she'd known him. Locksley was likely to catch hell for this, she thought in a panic. It would be all her fault.

"You!" Stainton cried out as he grabbed Fiona's arm. "You!" He seemed unable to find any other words for his fury. He yanked her to her feet, grabbed her fiddle, and smashed it into one of the rough wooden benches where they'd been sitting. "You are going to pay for this. Inciting nigger revolt is a crime in this colony." And with that, he swung her over his shoulder and carried her like a sack of potatoes to his quarters. And Fiona knew what punishment he had in mind.

Later, she wept, not for the rough sexual abuse that had again been perpetrated upon her. She had survived it once. She would survive again. She wept, not out of fear of being tried for inciting the blacks. She had done nothing of the sort. But she had broken a rather strict rule, even one Beatrice still adhered to, regardless of relenting to having black servants in the house and occasionally speaking to one of them.

No, she wept for the loss of her fiddle. It was like losing her Da, her lifeline to her homeland, her people. The major had taken the one thing she held dearer than almost anything else in life. This time, she wrote in her book all that took place. She drew a sketch of the major's face, contorted in his anger. He was an ugly man, in body, mind, and spirit.

She had again washed herself in the river after his attack, which was far more vicious this time, as he had also beaten her. He'd been careful not to bruise her face, but her back and arms were near to bloody. She again brewed her concoction of parsley and chamomile, praying to all the gods she could call upon, Christian or pagan, to wash away all residue of him from her body.

But by early June, it was apparent that the herbs had not worked. She dared pay a visit to the hoodoo woman in the Charlestown market one day when she accompanied Beatrice into town and purchased a potion from her that was to cleanse the female parts, using herbs harvested in the garden at Edgewater as barter.

Still, her condition remained the same, and she suffered the typical symptoms of the newly pregnant woman. By mid-July, her belly was beginning to round, and she gazed at it in the mirror, frightened and not knowing what to do. Major Stainton would likely murder her through some kind of "accident" if she told Beatrice. She wasn't sure what would happen if she did tell Beatrice, but she doubted it would result in forgiveness for either her or her husband.

"Alicia," she said one hot afternoon as they were wiping clean the noon meal dishes. "I need to talk to you."

"You with child, ain't you, Miss Fiona," Alicia said matter-of-factly. "The master got you that night, didn't he?"

Fiona was taken aback. "Why...yes, he did. And it was brutal."

"We all knew it was gon' happen. He's like that, taken many of our women to his room and done it to 'em. All them light-skinned babies out there in the village are his."

The ugly truth hit Fiona squarely between the eyes. Of course, he would do that. He owned those people, and he considered that he owned her as well. He could do as he wished with his "property." At this, she ran outside and wretched until there was nothing left for her to heave up. Alicia brought her a drink of water and led her to the low wall behind the kitchen. At last Fiona recovered sufficiently to speak again.

"What am I to do?" she asked, tears welling. "I did not ask for this. I did nothing that harmed him."

"Run," was all Alicia said.

"Run? Where? How? When?"

"Those traders will be back in town next month. The ones the master cheated, remember?"

So, she knew about that too. Locksley must have told his people what had really happened the night of the fire.

Alicia went on. "You not showin' much yet," she said. "You can take some time to plan it all out. Find the traders and go with them into th' high mountains. Master never find you there."

Over the coming weeks, Fiona forged a plan in her mind. It was dangerous, she knew, and she could be killed. She wasn't afraid of dying. She was more afraid of living once the Staintons found out her condition.

On the second day of September, Fiona had arranged to take Lady Stainton into Charlestown to be fitted for a new set of clothes. The night before, she packed her woolen satchel and stowed it under the seat of the carriage by the dark of night. Beneath her lady's maid attire, she wore the dress she'd had on when she left the ship. She'd determined that she'd not be accused of theft and planned to shed the clothing they'd bought for her and leave it all behind.

She left m'lady at the shop, giving her a look over her shoulder as she went out the door. She would miss her in a way. Beatrice had been kind to her, and in return, she had given Beatrice the gift of literacy, and perhaps that of greater self-assurance. But other than that, she'd been nothing more than a servant and had been subjected to a horror no woman should have to face, although she knew many had throughout time.

The carriage driver was a black man she knew from their good times at the frolics. She told him to look away as she retrieved her small satchel, removed her outer clothing, ducked behind the carriage, and ran for her life. She knew the traders hung out down by the warehouses at the wharf, and she was rewarded in her search.

"Mr. McNeill," she came upon him suddenly, and he jumped back.

"Who are you?" he said suspiciously.

At length, Fiona unwound her tale, fighting tears, and when McNeill found out who had done this to her, he hid her for the rest of the day in the shadows of the warehouse. "He's cheated us many times," she heard him tell one of the Indians. "It's only fair that we take something from him for a change."

That night, he and his Indians slipped out of town and headed northwest. Beneath a heavy blanket in the back of their wagon huddled a frightened, pregnant, but determined Irish girl with a stone talisman held tightly in her hand.

Chapter Thirty

The next day, Fiona came out of hiding at the invitation of Mr. McNeill. "You'll suffocate under there, girl," he said, and lifted the heavy canvas from her. Fiona looked around and blinked, scarcely believing she'd made her escape so easily. The sky was an ashen gray, and wind whipped her hair.

"Thank you, Mr. McNeill," she said as he helped her up to the wagon seat. Two Indians rode alongside, but they didn't turn their heads or look at her. Ahead, she saw another on horseback, and turning to look behind her, she saw a train of laden pack horses and three more Indians. "I hope I've not caused you any danger or trouble."

McNeill gave a rough laugh. "I'd like to see that old cheat try to follow us. He'd have an arrow in his heart before he knew what happened." He paused, then continued, "He won't be lookin' fer us. Not unless he comes across someone who saw you with us before we left, which is unlikely. I kept you hidden well."

Fiona hoped he was right. She knew if Major Stainton ever got his hands on her again, she would be a dead woman.

They rode in silence for a long while, Fiona chewing on her lip and considering her plight. She was here with a rough stranger and six Indians. There was no guarantee they wouldn't take her off into the woods, rape and murder her.

"Please, sir," she asked, "could you tell me where we are going?"

He gave her a grim smile, sensing her fears. "No worries, lass. I won't harm ye. But I'll find a good use for ye at Echoe."

"Echoe?"

"It's a Cherokee town. I have my trading business there. And a wife."

"You have a Cherokee wife?"

He laughed. "Oh, yes, and she'll find you quite useful, I'm sure."

A chill ran through her. She'd heard the Indians had slaves. Was she now to be a slave to a Cherokee? "Er, how so, Mr. McNeill?"

"The women in the town are the keepers of the earth," he said.

"Meaning, they do all the farming and raise the crops that feed the people. They can always use another hand."

Like Alicia and Arlevia worked the land on Stainton's plantation? "I must ask another question, sir. Am I then, well, a slave?"

He hesitated before replying, which in essence gave her the answer. Then he said, "Technically, yes. You won't be paid for your work, and someone will be telling you what to do. You will be punished if you fail to do as asked. But there's a difference between Indian slaves and those poor bastards down south, them black folk. Masters like Stainton treat their slaves like livestock. They own 'em, breed 'em, use 'em, sometimes kill 'em. It's not like that with the Cherokee. You'll be treated fairly, and you'll be fed and housed like one of them. Just don't try to run away," he added in warning.

They followed a trail that grew narrower the further they went from Charlestown. The Cherokee Trading Path, McNeill told her. He'd been trading furs for European goods for many years, acting as an agent going between the British and the Cherokee, and sometimes the Creeks and Catawbas, depending, he told her with a cheerless chuckle, on who was killing who at the moment. "They like to fight, the Indians do," he said. "It's in their blood. To my thinking, us whites are going to have to fight them at some time if we keep movin' into their land."

They made their way slowly, and the second day into their journey a strong storm with heavy rain, sometimes blown sideways by the force of the wind, hit them for several hours.

Taking refuge beneath the shelter of a large rock outcropping alongside the edge of the river they'd been following, the Indians built a fire, for which Fiona was grateful. She was chilled to the bone. She huddled by the fire and accepted a cup of coffee from McNeill. Absentmindedly, she had withdrawn the amulet from her pocket and was stroking it with her thumb when the old trader asked, "What's that then?"

Instinctively, she closed her fingers over it. "Nothing sir. Nothing but a pebble."

"A worry stone? You worried about something?"

She didn't know what a worry stone was, but she supposed she did call on it when she was worried. She managed a small laugh. "Now Mr. McNeill, what would I be worried about? You know my predicament, I'm in the middle of strange territory with men I barely know, going to live with the Indians. I can't imagine why I would be worried."

He nodded. "I understand, lass. I wasn't meanin' to make light of your situation. Can I see the stone? Does it hold magical powers?"

What an odd thing for him to say, Fiona thought, but reluctantly held it out for him to see.

He gave a low whistle, then summoned one of the Indians to come take a look. They turned the stone this way and that, speaking rapidly in the Cherokee tongue. At length Fiona had to ask, "What is wrong?"

"Where did you come by this, girl?" McNeill asked.

Surprised, Fiona blinked. "Why, my Granny gave it to me as I left Ireland. 'Tis engraved with some ancient Irish symbols. I don't know if they are magical. I doubt it, but it gives me comfort when, as you say, I am worried or unhappy." Then she added, "Why do you ask?"

The Indian appeared to be very agitated, and he spoke in his own language to McNeill, pointing to Fiona almost accusingly. But McNeill shook his head, and she discerned his reply satisfied the Indian, at least for the moment.

"What is it, Mr. McNeill?" she pressed.

"It's very strange," he said, returning the stone to her. "There is a large stone, a boulder really, further west in Creek territory, that carries these same symbols. Legend has it that it was carved by some ancient people who lived around here, the 'painted people' whose hair was red and skin was light, with eyes the sky color." He squinted and surveyed her. "Like yours," he added.

"What's that to do with me?"

"The painted people were early Creeks, the mortal enemies of the Cherokee," he said, and she detected a concern in his tone.

"He doesn't think I'm a Creek or even an Indian, does he?"

After a long pause, Mr. McNeill replied, "I'd just keep that stone out of sight if I was you."

A few days later, they arrived at a village called Keowee, where they camped and rested. Fiona learned that this thriving village was one of several others known as the Cherokee Lower Towns. Callum McNeill was a wealth of information about these people, and in spite of her fear and trepidation about her uncertain future with them, she was also fascinated by them. To her eyes, they were peaceful. Their village was ordered, people spoke to one another in friendly tones, and she was treated with deference after McNeill said she was with him and would be his wife's property.

The first night they were there, an Indian woman approached and spoke to Fiona, words she could not understand, but they did not seem threatening. "I...I'm sorry," she stuttered, "but I do not know your language."

McNeill was nearby. "She's inviting you to sleep in her home," he said pleasantly. "I would take her up on it if I were you."

As she joined the woman inside the small log cabin, Fiona saw a large cast iron pot hanging over a fire in a stone hearth, and a delicious aroma met her nose. She hadn't eaten much since they set out on their journey, and her stomach issued forth a loud growl, at which both women looked at one another, and then laughed.

After they had dined, the woman led Fiona back outside to a central square where a large bonfire burned, reminiscent of the one in the slave village. The natives began their own version of a "frolic," with dancing and music played on cane flutes and water drums, with shells providing the rhythm as they shook from the anklets worn by the woman dancers. Suddenly there was a cry from a lookout at the edge of the village, and all the young men who only moments before had been dancing as if totally carefree grabbed weapons and ran toward the warning sound. Fiona heard shouts and a lone, confused and agonized cry. Moments later, the braves returned to the fire, dragging with them a young black girl.

"Alicia!" Fiona screamed and ran to her. "Let her go," she cried out to her captors. "Let her go!"

Callum McNeill stepped in to prevent further mayhem. "What is this?" he demanded.

"She's my friend. She's...she must have run away from Major Stainton too." Fiona turned to Alicia and peered into her frightened eyes. "Is that what you've done, Alicia?"

The girl nodded. "That day you left, there was trouble. The master brought all the slaves together and demanded someone tell him where you went. But we didn't know. I'm the only one who knew you'd run away, but I didn't know where."

She showed Fiona her back which was slashed from the whipping he'd given her. "He even whipped Locksley," she said, starting to cry.

Fiona was shocked and horrified, and she didn't know what to say, but Alicia wasn't finished. "The day after you left it turned a big storm. Bigger than the one we had on the ocean," she said. "Monster storm. Tore our village apart, broke down the big house. Flooded everywhere. Must have destroyed Charlestown if it went there too."

"Oh my God," Fiona uttered. "What about Mrs. Stainton? Is she all right?"

Alicia continued to blubber. "No, m'am. She dead. The master made Locksley board her up in that house, and when it crashed, it came down 'round her head."

Fiona could stand it no more. She pulled Alicia into her arms and cradled her head and rocked her gently. "Your mama?" she asked after a moment.

Alicia looked up with wide, tear-filled eyes, then looked around at the Indians and Mr. McNeill. "Safe here?" she asked.

Fiona asked that of Mr. McNeill, who although bewildered at this turn of affairs, spoke to the chief of the village, who assured him the girl would not be harmed. Alicia wriggled free from Fiona's embrace and turned and faced the darkness from whence she had come. She whistled loudly, three sharp notes, and in moments, two other black figures appeared within the light of the fire, one carrying a small child.

Fiona was stunned. "Locksley! Arlevia!" And she ran to them.

Behind her, McNeill wiped his brow. "Just what I need. Runaway slaves."

Chapter Thirty-One

Echoe, Cherokee Middle Town, Spring 1754

The morning was fresh and cool, and the sunlight filtering through the trees in the mountain forest seemed to Fiona as if it was streaming directly from the heavens. She was in the woods, gathering wild onions and herbs with other women from the village. It had been more than a year since she fled Charlestown, and in that time, she had come to have a deeper appreciation of the natural world from observing the lives and customs of the native people who had taken her in.

It had not been easy, coming to live in a world so alien to anything she had ever known, among people whose lives seemed in many ways as if they were from another, much earlier age. Their homes, although adequate, were more primitive even than her lowly cottage in Ireland. They cultivated the neighboring fields without the use of the farm tools her Da had used and that she'd seen on the plantation. They cooked over open fires, mostly outside of the dwellings, and although she'd seen a few families with iron pots or kettles acquired from the English traders, much of their kitchen ware was of handmade pottery. Although they had also obtained guns and ammunition from traders, many still used blow guns and bows and arrows for hunting. She didn't distain any of this, but she found the disparity in lifestyles between what she'd seen in Charlestown and here unsettling. No wonder the Indians wanted what the white man was able to deliver, things more modern and effective, especially guns.

Nor was her reception by them exactly welcoming. She recalled the day they arrived in Echoe, and McNeill presented his wife, Ma-ri, with the new slaves. She took one look at Fiona's belly and let out a horrific shriek and began pounding on McNeill's chest in fury. Fiona understood not a word, but it wasn't hard to guess that Ma-ri was accusing McNeill of fathering her child.

The trader had shaken his head and taken his wife by both wrists, holding her steady until she calmed down somewhat, all the while saying "no, no, no!" Meanwhile other villagers circled around them, curious to see what was going on. McNeill spoke to her in Cherokee, obviously denying her accusations, but Ma-ri was not easily placated. She continued to rage, then grew quiet. She slowly raised her head and said something that made McNeill's face turn white. He replied, "No. Please. Ma-ri. No."

But she'd pulled away from him and ducked inside the log cabin that was her home. Fiona stared at McNeill. "What happened?"

"She said she is going to divorce me."

"What? Just like that?"

"It's their way," McNeill said, scratching his head and turning away, going back to his wagon. "The women can marry and divorce as many times as they like."

"But she didn't give you a chance," Fiona protested, incensed that someone would believe she would take up with a fellow like the scruffy Callum McNeill. But for all Ma-ri knew, McNeill could have done to Fiona exactly what Stainton had done. "Isn't there any recourse?"

"Maybe."

She'd followed McNeill to the center of the village where stood a large, seven-sided structure, their council house. Along the way, he was greeted by a number of the men who recognized him and who murmured what seemed to be condolences. They also stared unabashedly at Fiona. At the entrance to the building, McNeill asked the bare-breasted brave who stood guard outside the doorway if he could speak to Unika, whom she later learned was the chief of this village. He waited outside the building until the guard beckoned him inside. Fiona started to follow, but the guard stepped in her path and ordered her to leave. He spoke in Cherokee, but his message was pretty clear.

She turned away from the doorway to find the entire village staring at her. Cheeks burning, she quickly fled back to McNeill's wagon, not knowing where else to go. Sorely frightened, she'd clutched her Granny's amulet until her knuckles turned white.

A while later, McNeill returned to his wagon. "You're to be housed for now with the nigras in a cabin recently vacated by the death of its occupant," he told her. His face was unreadable, but he appeared agitated.

"What about you...and your wife?"

"The chief is her father. I explained to him what happened, and how you came to be with me. I think he plans to speak to Ma-ri. We will have to see if she will believe him."

"I'm sorry, Mr. McNeill," Fiona said. "I never meant..."

But he'd cut her short. "'Tis not your fault," he told her brusquely. "'Tis the life of a trader to come and go. Not exactly the life a wife would relish, according to Unika. Perhaps this is just her excuse to get rid of me and marry one of her own kind who is home more than I have been."

Pausing in the forest on this quiet spring morning, she reflected on the past year, which had been terrifying and challenging. But after hearing from Locksley what transpired after she fled Edgewater, she never looked back. According to him, the huge storm hit early the morning after they'd left, the same day, Fiona reckoned, that she and the trader's convoy had taken shelter beneath the rocks on the river.

"It was fiercesome, Miss Fiona," Locksley told her. "The storm blew Stainton Hall to pieces, and a heavy beam fell on Lady Stainton, killing her." According to Locksley's account, when the storm passed, upon learning of his wife's death, Major Stainton didn't mourn her loss or that of his house. He gave Locksley terse instructions to bury Beatrice at the back of the garden, then left immediately for Charlestown to check on his businesses there. Fiona could only assume that the ugly bastard was glad Beatrice was gone, because her death would be considered an "act of God," and his claim on her dowry would be forever secured.

In Echoe, Fiona and the Africans had been led to a log cabin not unlike the one Ma-ri lived in, and McNeill brought her battered woolen satchel from his wagon. There were few furnishings inside the cabin—two beds made of logs and covered with blankets, a bench, and fireplace tools by the hearth.

McNeill left them then, and they just stared at one another in silence, not knowing what to do next.

Shortly, however, several women had arrived with wood to build a fire, ears of corn, a basket of beans, and a type of gourd. They were silent, and none would so much as glance at them. A man brought a large iron pot and bridle to suspend it above the fire and was followed by a woman bearing a pottery container of water. Instinctively, Fiona said, "Thank you," and then realized the Indians probably would not understand her. But one of them, a pretty young woman, turned to her and smiled. "*Gvlieliga*," she replied, and then added shyly. "You welcome."

Fiona had smiled, relieved to learn that someone here spoke at least a bit of English. But then she remembered that McNeill traded with these people and was married to one of them. He had obviously learned their language, and it stood to reason that some of them had learned his. But she noted that the young woman was chastised by the others for having spoken to her.

After the first night in the village, a tall, elderly man dressed in a flowing robe and wearing many beaded ornaments had come to the cabin and spoken to Fiona. "You come with me." She'd been terrified but since she had no choice, she gathered her courage and followed him, glancing over her shoulder at her African friends, wondering if she'd ever see them again. He led her past Ma-ri's cabin, where she saw McNeill standing in the doorway, smoking a pipe. He grinned at her and gave a sign that all was well.

They'd arrived at a larger cabin close to the center of the village, and the man indicated for her to enter. Inside, it was dark except for a small fire that burned in the fireplace, and smoke pervaded the room. A woman whose age Fiona couldn't tell, although her long hair was mostly silver, sat by the hearth. "Nanyeh, I bring you a gift," the man spoke in English. He took Fiona by both shoulders and gently guided her toward the woman.

The woman spoke back in Cherokee, and the two conversed at length, then the woman nodded and indicated for him to leave them. Fiona guessed she was now this woman's slave, since Ma-ri obviously did not want her.

"Come. Sit," the woman said quietly, indicating for Fiona to take a seat on a deerskin rug nearby.

"Thank you," was all Fiona could think of to say, and she sat down.

"I know your story," Nanyeh said in surprisingly good English. She pointed to Fiona's swelling belly. "It was not McNeill who did this to you, but another, very bad, man."

Fiona had lived with terror and apprehension for so many months, suddenly her pent-up emotions spilled over, and she began to weep. She didn't even try to hold back the tears. She knew not why, but she felt as if she could trust this woman, as if they were kindred spirits. "Yes," she sobbed. "A very bad man. I ran away, and McNeill saved my life. But he has never touched me."

"Ma-ri is my daughter," Nanyeh told her. "She has a hot head, but she loves McNeill. Her father has set her straight, I believe."

Fiona raised her head, sniffled, and managed a smile. "I am glad for that."

"You are to live with me and Unika now," Nanyeh had told her. Fiona learned that the man who had brought her to this woman was the chief, and she was his wife. She was also the village's *ghighau*, their beloved woman, their war woman, and their healer. Fiona sensed that she held great power among her people.

Nanyeh had grown silent and gazed for a long while into the fire before speaking again, as if she were searching the flames for answers to her unspoken questions. Then she turned and said, "I see you are a spirit woman, like myself, but from another world. You have much to learn here. I have been shown by our spirit elders that I am to help you, but you must become one with our people."

It had taken more than a year, but under Nanyeh's sponsorship and her own diligence, Fiona had slowly been accepted by these people. Their village was small, and the villagers, who lived in a remote valley surrounded by high mountains, were reticent with outsiders. She had learned some of the Cherokee language, and although it was still difficult for her to pronounce, her efforts had gained respect among them. She and the Africans worked as slaves, but it was as McNeill had told them, they were treated well and worked alongside the Indians, not just for them.

What had made a big difference in gaining their acceptance was music. Fiona had heard one of the tribesmen playing a haunting melody on a flute the Cherokee made from river cane and asked if she could try playing it. The man handed it to her with a grin that was almost a challenge, as if daring her to make music with it. The instrument was different from Mr. Bentley's Irish flute, and it took her some time to master it, but the man she'd borrowed it from, seemingly impressed, gave it to her, indicating he could make another.

She practiced in the privacy of her cabin, experimenting with tunes she knew from her homeland. One night she joined some merrymaking around a fire, where she watched the men and women perform circle dances, and music filled the air. She had practiced playing the Indian-style flute enough to feel confident with it, and when there was a lull between dances, she started piping a spirited jig like Mr. Bentley had done on board. The Indians grew silent and stared at her in astonishment, but in a moment, one of them, the one who'd barred her from the doorway when they'd arrived, grinned broadly and started moving his feet in time to the rhythm. Nanyeh was quick to pick up the beat, clapping her hands, and as these two appeared to support Fiona's effort to play music, others from the village began to participate, playing drums and shaking rattles. Alicia and her mother joined in the frolic, and from that night on, things had been easier for her and her African friends.

As Fiona's pregnancy advanced, Nanyeh had guided her in the Cherokee way of preparing for a safe birthing: what foods she was to eat, what foods she must avoid. She bathed daily in the nearby river. Some ceremonies she didn't understand but participated in them because for the first time since she'd left her home in Ireland, she felt cherished and cared for. Nanyeh, in some ways, was like her Granny.

It was Nanyeh who, on a cold day in February more than a year ago, was with Fiona when her labor began. She'd brewed an infusion of wild cherry bark to hasten the delivery and performed the Cherokee rituals to insure a safe birth. She added wood to the fire and placed clean reed mats on the ground to receive the child. Then she and two other women from the tribe showed Fiona the Cherokee way of giving birth and aided her in squatting and pushing, letting nature and gravity help. It was Nanyeh who first saw the red hair of the baby boy as he left the womb, who caught him and placed him gently on the bed of reeds.

"Firehead!" she exclaimed, giving Aidan Cassidy II his Cherokee name.

CHAPTER THIRTY-TWO

They lived a peaceful life for the most part, but Fiona had no illusions. She knew the Indians could be as fierce as their reputation. She had heard angry speeches given around the council fires by warriors who had traveled from other villages to share the news of the encroachment of white settlers onto their lands. It seemed the French, too, were stirring up trouble. From what she could understand, France and England were at war, and that war was making its way into the back country of this new land. Both sides, she reckoned, wanted these natives, whose land they were taking away little by little, to fight for them.

But today, surrounded by tall, ancient trees in this mountain forest, all of that seemed far away and of little importance to her. She was with Nanyeh, Alicia, and several other women of the village, harvesting the strong-smelling plant that somewhat resembled a small white onion that grew in the forest in springtime. Nanyeh had shown her the Cherokee way of taking what they needed from the earth but leaving enough that the plant would regenerate and provide for them again next year. "Take one, leave three."

Fiona found the Cherokee ways much like the old ways her Granny had taught her in Ireland. Nanyeh knew the healing nature of many plants. Some were familiar to Fiona, others that grew here in the mountains were new to her . She kept careful records of these plants in her small book that was rapidly filling up. She would ask McNeill to bring her a new one on his next trading journey.

Fiona shared her own knowledge of healing plants, showing Nanyeh the drawings in her notebook and giving her use of the dried herbs she'd managed to bring with her. She quickly grew to love and respect this Cherokee elder woman, who had helped her learn the spiritual ways of her people and brought her into the community as other than a slave. But sometimes she wasn't sure if her feelings were returned. It was apparent that unlike the Irish, the Cherokee were reserved and did not readily show emotion, except when it came to war. Nanyeh was soft-spoken, but Fiona found she had a rather bawdy sense of humor, and she loved to gossip. And she was kind. And that was enough.

This morning, as the women went about their search for the wild onions, Firehead was asleep under a tree in the cradleboard Nanyeh's son, Ma-ri's brother Onacona, or White Owl, had made for him. Since Fiona had no husband, Nanyeh and her clan family had placed the boy in this man's care, as it was the custom among them for the mother's brother to take on the guidance and education of her son. Fiona wondered at the time if that made her relationship to Nanyeh one of mother and daughter, but she dared not ask.

Fiona stood to place a handful of the smelly onions in her harvest basket and took a moment to look at her sleeping little boy. He was just over a year old now and soon would walk. She was amused that they called him Firehead, but in truth, she was glad that his hair had come in thick and red, although not as curly as her own. She had been afraid he would look like the loathsome man who had sired him and was grateful that instead he reminded her of her own Da.

The longer she lived among the Indians, the easier it was for her to try to forget how Aidan had been conceived, but sometimes in her nightmares, she saw images of that large gold watch Nigel Stainton had placed on his desk and which had loomed in her sight both times he'd raped her. To her, the watch symbolized Stainton, and she would never forget it.

She'd learned from McNeill that, unfortunately, Nigel Stainton had not only survived the hurricane but in fact had benefitted from the reconstruction of Charlestown. He was a friend of the governor now, and according to the trader, remained solid in his hatred of the native people. Fiona hoped her son would never know his real father, but she was at a loss as to what to say to him when one day he asked, as he most surely would. She didn't believe in lying, so in her heart and her mind, she killed Nigel Stainton. He was dead to her now, and so she would tell Aidan that he had died and let that be that.

If only it were true.

* * *

Late Summer, 1756

Life in the village was pleasant for Fiona and Firehead as the little *usdi* grew strong and sturdy. Onacona, who was unmarried, visited Fiona's cabin often, on the pretext of his responsibilities to Aidan, but she sensed there was more to his motives. The attention he showed her was not exactly "brotherly." She found him attractive, in a wild sort of way. He was tall and well-muscled, and he seldom wore a shirt. He was the man who had been standing guard at the council house that first day they arrived, keeping watch over his father's domain. It was obvious that he was respected among the villagers, and when he was with her, the people seemed comically curious of their relationship. As far as she was concerned, he was the "uncle" in charge of the boy, and nothing more.

She and the Africans had been released from their position as slaves and became part of the tribe, as if adopted. Locksley had proven to be as useful to the chief and other tribal members as he had been to the major and was treated with more respect than he'd known on the plantation. He and Arlevia had married in a Cherokee ceremony and moved with Alicia and Abe into a house of their own. Alicia was sought after by more than one young warrior, but she remained aloof and inscrutable as to her desires.

Fiona and Aidan also moved into a cabin which she shared from time to time with Quella Longtree, Nanyeh's sister who traveled much of the time. Quella was an interesting companion, and Fiona looked forward to her visits. "The Great Spirit put rocks in my moccasins," she'd told Fiona once. "That's what makes me always want to move."

Quella told Fiona her story: after the death of her husband in a fierce battle with the Creeks, she had spent time alone in the high mountains far to the north in Virginia, seeking spiritual healing. There she'd encountered white settlers who had moved to the far edges of what was allowed by treaty. Maybe even beyond the edges. But as a medicine woman, she had taken care of them, and in fact, they called her a 'granny woman,' their name for someone who was something between a mystical healer and midwife. Despite her Indian blood, they came to trust her for her knowledge of herbal medicines and her skills in bringing babies into the world. Between Nanyeh and Quella, Fiona learned much about life on this far frontier and living in her in-between world, a white woman in a red man's land.

Quella didn't hate the whites, as some of her tribe did. Nor did she trust them. She told Fiona that she knew in her heart the white man wanted all Indians dead, or at least removed from these, their ancestral lands. Her words were heart-rending to Fiona, who remembered the pain she'd felt when her Da had told her of the English plans to force young Irish people out of their homeland to serve as slaves in the Caribbean. How distressed she'd been watching the blacks in Africa, stolen from their homes, pried at gunpoint onto the slave ship.

Although the villagers treated her as one of them now, there were times when she longed to be with others of her own kind. She doubted that would ever be, however, and allowed Aidan to be raised like other Indian boys. Except in cold weather, he went about unclad, as all the young children did. He'd learned many words in Cherokee, and Onacona had already given him a tiny bow and arrow and taught him how to shoot it.

Fiona had mixed emotions about her Irish lad learning to become an Indian. Although she spoke to him in English, he spoke Cherokee to Onacona and others of the clan. Once, when some dark-haired Indian boys teased him about his red hair, his temper rose, and he lashed out at his tormentors, who came away worse for the encounter, one with a broken nose. He was learning to stand up for himself, and Fiona struggled to let him find his own way, as she was advised by Onacona. "He must learn to be a man," he'd told her. White Owl introduced Firehead to the Cherokee ways of hunting and fishing, and in spite of his youth, the boy was learning the secrets of the forests and mountains. Fiona could see the pride Onacona took in tutoring the child in the customs of his people, and she saw in turn how Aidan loved and respected this man.

One day in late spring a group of Cherokee warriors from a village in the Overhill towns came galloping into the center of the town, shouting and whooping, and all the villagers ran to the council house. "This can only mean trouble," Nanyeh said as she and Fiona joined the rest.

The warriors were all young, and it was apparent to Fiona that they were here to raise some kind of alarm. That, or like Nanyeh predicted, to cause trouble. She'd heard that many of the younger Cherokees wanted the chance to go to war, to earn their honor through bloody victory. It made no sense to her, but Nanyeh had told her it had been the way of the Cherokee people for as long as they had lived in these mountains, and for other tribes as well. They were mortal enemies of the Creeks and the Shawnees in particular.

Unika approached as the young warriors dismounted, with Onacona right behind him, spear in hand. They came to Unika as a group, then one among them, a young man with a severely pock-marked face, stepped to the forefront and acknowledged Unika as chief. He spoke rapidly and angrily in Cherokee, and it was impossible for Fiona to follow what he said. She whispered to Nanyeh to translate.

"He says, 'We come from Chota and Settico to tell of more betrayals by the English and bloodshed of our brothers murdered by white men in Virginia. It is time for all Cherokees to fight the lying English and take back our lands.'"

The old chief ushered them into the council house, and the entire village entered behind them. As was their custom, the chief took his place by the fire, and Nanyeh, as the beloved and war woman, sat next to him. Their son, Onacona, stood behind his father. Fiona took a seat on one of the benches that lined the sides of the structure and listened intently, trying to understand what had happened.

After the young brave finished what was a long and impassioned oratory, he turned and faced the young men of the Echoe village and shouted something that brought cheers and war whoops from them. The visiting tribesmen then left the council house, and the villagers, including Fiona, followed them.

She was distracted by what had been said, at least the part she could understand, when suddenly she was seized by one of the Overhill warriors, and before she knew what happened, he had grabbed her by both wrists with one hand, and in the other, he pulled at her hair, which had by now grown quite long and was worn in a single braid like the Indian women.

"*Yo! Ni!*" he cried. "English!" And then he spoke in English. "Frenches pay well for this scalp!" he shouted with glee.

Fiona yanked her hands free as he went for his scalping knife. She tried to wrest his hand from her hair, but he was strong, and his manner was wild. For a moment, she thought she was about to die and lose her red hair in the process.

Onacona rushed to them and placed his own knife beneath her attacker's throat. "No. She is ours. You don't touch her, or her boy. They belong to us."

The visiting warrior was startled at first, but he quickly let go of her hair and backed away, hatred in his eyes. He said something to her rescuer that she took as either an insult or a threat, or possibly both, but the leader of his party came and pulled him away, admonishing him in Cherokee.

Fiona stood for a moment, trying to catch her breath and slow her hammering heart. Then she looked at Onacona and nodded. "*Wado udohiyu utsati*, my friend," she said to him. "Thank you very much." Then she turned and ran as fast as she could back to her cabin, where Alicia was tending to both Aidan and her little brother Abe. Fiona sank to the floor and began to shake as she shared her terror with her African friend.

A little while later, Nanyeh came to the cabin, and while she brewed a calming herbal drink for Fiona, she related what had transpired in the council house. "That was Dragging Canoe speaking," she said. "He is the son of the main peace chief Ada-gal'kala, but this one wants no peace. He says the British came to the Overhill towns and encouraged Cherokee warriors to go north with the British to fight the Shawnees, who have aligned with the French. In turn, they said they would build a fort nearby to protect the women and children while they were gone. But the timing was bad. The British thought if they went in January, not a normal time of year to wage war, they would have the advantage of surprise in attacking the Shawnee."

She moved to pour her brew into a cup, which she handed to Fiona and indicated for her to drink. "It will settle you," she said, then she continued. "It was they who received the surprise instead when the canoes that carried all their supplies and ammunition hit an ice jam and were lost in the river. Those who survived came ashore and met up with the ones who'd traveled by horseback. But with everything washed away, there was no point in them going on with the plan."

"How terrible," Fiona murmured, feeling the warm liquid starting to calm her nerves.

"Yes. But the warriors had no food, and so on their return home, they had to kill their horses to eat. When the animals were gone, the group came upon a farm in Virginia, and finding no one home to offer help, they took what they needed for food and also stole some horses."

Fiona could tell this wasn't a story with a happy ending. She waited for Nanyeh to continue.

"The Virginians, upon discovering their loss, ambushed the returning warriors and killed twenty-three Cherokees. Now, Dragging Canoe wants vengeance. He plans to kill twenty-three white people to pay for the lives of the men who were killed."

Fiona was astounded. "Just any twenty-three people? Or those who did the killing?"

"It matters not. It was white people who killed the Cherokees. White people must pay, according to the Cherokee old ways."

Fiona shivered. It was this part of their culture that she not only didn't understand but also found horrifying.

She later learned that Dragging Canoe had indeed taken a raiding party back into Virginia, where they had killed twenty-three whites, none of whom likely had anything to do with the killing of the Cherokees. The whites were killed at random as the raiders came upon them until they reached the number twenty-three. Having claimed the revenge he sought, Dragging Canoe ceased the killing and returned home. But Fiona heard rumors that others, perhaps inspired by his actions, had begun to raid and murder white settlers all the way from Virginia through North Carolina and into South Carolina. The violence of it all made her head swim, and she could only hope that she and Aidan would somehow avoid falling victim to these murderous ways. Onacona had saved her scalp once, but she knew her hair, and that of her son, were mighty tempting targets for any who would kill a white person just because of the color of her skin.

CHAPTER THIRTY-THREE

A few days later, Fiona was busy shucking the corn she and others had brought in from the fields next to the village, the last of this year's harvest, when she was startled to see the chief, Unika, approaching her cabin, with Nanyeh close behind. She stood up and brushed the corn silk from her skirt and greeted them warmly. "*Osiyo.*"

Nanyeh rushed past her husband, and the look on her face told Fiona that something urgent was about to happen. "My husband has come with news," she said. "But it may not be to your liking."

Fiona looked around, wondering if something had happened to little Firehead, but she saw him playing happily with his best friend Dustu and two other boys nearby. She moved to one side of the bench she'd been sitting on and invited them to take a seat, but Unika remained standing.

"Onacona has come to me," he said in his deep, rich voice. "He wants permission to marry you. Since you have no mother here, Nanyeh has offered to arrange it for the both of you."

Fiona blinked. Marry? She was fond of Onacona, but not in that way. In many respects, she hardly knew him. She turned to Nanyeh. "I...I'm not ready to be married," she stammered. "I like Onacona well enough, but..." She stopped short of saying she didn't want to marry an Indian.

Somewhere in the back of her mind and heart, she still longed to be among her own people.

"Take some time to consider it," Nanyeh said. "Our son has told us he has deep feelings for you, and for your boy." Fiona saw a twinkle in the older woman's eye. "You could do worse. He is the son of the chief, might become chief himself someday. He has horses to offer you, as well as his life. And," she reminded Fiona, "the spirit elders spoke of you becoming one with our people. Perhaps this is what they meant."

Fiona swallowed hard. She could see that this woman, her friend and spiritual guide, wanted this very much for her son. She looked up at the chief, but his face was inscrutable. Taking a deep breath, she said, "I am honored at this offer, Chief Unika. But I don't know your son well enough to become his wife at this time."

"Find time to be with him," the old man replied. "You will come to know him. He has a strong spirit, like you. You belong together."

Fiona didn't think she belonged together with anyone other than her son, but his words struck a chord. A strong spirit... She had found Onacona attractive, and he had always been gentle and respectful of her. She would turn twenty years old come December, and her hopes of ever returning to the world she'd left behind were dimming each day. "I will think about it," she said before realizing the commitment that she made. She should just say no but found she could not. "I will, as you suggest, find time to be with him and get to know his spirit."

Satisfied, Unika turned to leave, but Fiona added, "That doesn't mean I will marry him, though." Unika's back straightened visibly, but he said nothing more and left the cabin.

Fiona turned to find Nanyeh laughing silently. "No one stands up to him like you just did," she said, not scolding but in fact with a bit of admiration. "No one except Onacona, who reveres his father but does not always agree with him."

* * *

Early autumn in the mountains brought cooler nights that foretold the coming cold weather, but the days remained warm and pleasant. On such a day, shortly after Unika's visit, Fiona heard a knock and found Onacona at her doorstep. He handed her a bunch of wildflowers and grinned shyly, almost boyishly, although he was several years older than she. "Father says you wish to get to know my spirit."

Fiona had fretted about what might come of her conversation with his parents, and now here he was boldly courting her. "I...I don't know, Onacona. You have been a good friend and uncle to my son. This changes everything between us, and I'm not sure I want to lose what we have."

He didn't move or lose his composure. "It could make it better, Fiona. Will you walk with me this morning?"

Searching for a good reason not to, Fiona said, "I have no one to look after Aidan."

"He can come with us. I know him well and have been almost like a father to him," he reminded her. At that moment, Firehead popped out the door and into Onacona's arms.

"White Owl! Can we go hunting?"

Onacona looked at Fiona, who only shrugged, her only excuse now gone. Onacona said, "We will go hunting for more than a deer," and he tousled Aidan's his red hair. "Maybe we'll find something for your mother."

* * *

The October leaves were as fiery red as the hair on Fiona's head the day she wed Onacona. It wasn't an easy decision, but he'd been persistent, and she had found it in her heart to try to learn to love him as a husband. She had "walked with him" numerous times, and she learned that he was torn about the loss of Cherokee land to the whites, but he wasn't like Dragging Canoe. He had hopes that someday the two would be able to enjoy peaceful co-existence. She'd learned that he liked being Aidan's teacher, and that he truly loved her son. And then one day, when she at last allowed him to kiss her, she realized that she loved him. She truly did, and she decided then and there that it no longer mattered to her that he was Indian.

Somehow Quella had learned of the upcoming ceremony and arrived a few days before the wedding bearing a lovely white deerskin dress embellished with many beads. "For you, with wishes for a happy union." As she accepted the magnificent gift, Fiona saw the doubt in Quella's troubled eyes.

Doubt? Or premonition?

"*Wado*," she said, taking the garment from Quella and laying it gently on a bench nearby. Then she asked, "Am I making a mistake?"

Quella remained silent for a long time, then replied, "These are difficult times. It will not be easy for you, nor for him, this marriage. But if you love each other and are willing to face this uncertain future together, then it is not a mistake." She gave Fiona a hug, then added, "One must take happiness when and where one can. This I wish for you and Onacona."

The wedding ceremony was a simple one. The villagers, including her soon-to-be in-laws Ma-ri and McNeill, gathered in the central square in front of the council house surrounding the sacred fire.

Nanyeh, as the village's beloved woman, blessed the couple, then turned and blessed all the guests. Then according to Cherokee custom, Fiona presented her new husband with a basket of corn, a symbol that she would be a good Cherokee wife, and also acknowledging her role as a woman of the tribe to tend to the crops and the land. Onacona in turn presented her with a haunch of venison, symbolically promising to provide for her in every way. The pair turned to stand shoulder to shoulder, and Unika covered them with a blanket, uniting them in marriage.

After the ceremony, the couple drank from a pottery wedding vase that had two openings for them to drink at the same time from the same cup. And then they were done. Fiona and Onacona were husband and wife. Although she had agreed to this, and for the most part was happy, she had some consolation that if it didn't work out, she could do as Ma-ri had threatened to do to McNeill, and divorce him by simply placing his belongings outside the door to her cabin. For it was her cabin, not his. This was one aspect of Cherokee life that she found gratifying. It was a society in which women held power.

CHAPTER THIRTY-FOUR

Echoe, Cherokee Middle Town, June 1760

Fiona sat by the fire, her young daughter Maura, now almost three, on her lap and seven-year-old Aidan by her side. They watched as the kernels of hard dried corn sizzled at the bottom of the big pot and began one by one to pop open into small, white buds. Maura laughed and clapped her tiny hands, and Fiona was filled with joy to hear her children squeal in delight. They were about to empty the pot into bowls to enjoy this treat when Onacaona rushed through the doorway.

"Come!" he said urgently to his wife. "There is news." He took her by the hand and pulled her to her feet, picked up Maura, and beckoned Aidan to follow them to the council house.

"What's happened?" Fiona asked, breathless at this sudden intrusion.

"They're coming."

"Who?"

"English soldiers."

Inside the council house, the villagers gathered solemnly to hear the grisly details of an attack on the Cherokee Lower Towns perpetrated by the English and the colonists in South Carolina. "They burned the villages to the ground, killed many, took many prisoners." The messenger was a survivor of that attack, and he was with a raggedy band of others who'd manage to escape. "They plan to march through here on their way to Fort Loudoun to free their soldiers being held there by our tribe, in retribution for our young and reckless warriors' killing of their soldiers at Fort Prince George."

This was the first Fiona had heard of this particular conflict between the English and the Indians, although she'd heard of many instances when both the Indians and the white settlers, most of whom were English, had attacked and killed one another. At first, she was confused, thinking the English and the Cherokee were allies, but the

Cherokee had changed after that winter disaster that ended in brutal bloodshed on both sides. She drew her children close. Retribution begat retribution, she'd learned, and the English participated in the despicable practice as much as the Indians, a practice no one could win.

After listening to more details of the attack, Unika held up his hand for silence. "We have known this could happen," he said. "Ada'gal'kala was through here recently on his way to South Carolina to attempt once more to make peace with the English. But their governor no longer wants peace. And he wants more than our prisoners at Fort Loudoun." He paused, then added gravely, "He wants us all dead. He wants our nation destroyed so the white man can move freely upon our ancestral lands."

At this, an angry murmur spread among the villagers. "We must fight them!" one cried out, and his shout was followed by many others in agreement. Some even began to make the turkey gobble sound that was a war cry. But again, Unika held up his hand.

"Our tribesmen here have brought us warning, but we have little time to prepare." Then the old chief ordered all able-bodied men to remain with him inside the council house to discuss plans as to how best to stand and fight. The women, children and elderly were ordered to make plans to leave their homes and hide in the forest until the danger passed.

Fiona guided her children out of the building and sought out Nanyeh. "What is your advice?" she asked the elder woman.

Nanyeh turned sad eyes on Fiona. "We must do as Unika bids," she answered. "He has spoken to me of this possibility, and we have agreed that to save our tribe, we must both fight and flee. I am to guide the villagers to safety, and he will remain with the warriors. As he says, we haven't much time, if what the messenger said is true. Go now and prepare. We must leave quickly."

Returning to her cabin, Fiona crumpled into a chair, drawing her children into her arms. "What is it, Ma?" Aidan asked. "What did those men mean? And where is Onacona?"

"He is with his father and the other men of the village." She drew in a heavy breath. "We are about to come upon bad times, little

Firehead," she said, using his Cherokee name. Even as she said it, she wondered what would happen if they ended up in the hands of the English. How would they treat her and her children, especially Maura, who was half-breed? Suddenly she thought of Alicia, and Locksley, Arlevia and Abe. Runaway slaves. They wouldn't stand a chance, and she knew it. Nanyeh was right.

They must run, all of them. Unika's words echoed in her mind, *He wants us all dead. He wants our nation destroyed so the white man can move freely upon our ancestral lands*. Words almost identical to something Quella had said years ago.

Must she always keep running? Fiona wondered suddenly, and her fear turned to anger. Was there no peace to be found in this so-called wonderful New World into which she'd been thrust? But running was nothing new to her, and she released her children and reached for the woolen satchel that had been her only constant companion on her journeys.

Journeys!

The tea leaves had foretold she would have more than one journey the night before she left Ireland. What had Granny told her that night? *You will be needed, Fiona.*

She considered her children. One the child of rape, the other a half-breed Indian. Yes, they needed her, as did Nanyeh and the other villagers. And the time was now.

Taking only her satchel, a rifle, as much food as she could carry, and her children, Fiona joined the other women, children, and old people as they tearfully left their village, some on horseback but most on foot, with their horses bearing the burden of their meager belongings. The corn was just beginning to ripen in the fields, and peaches hung in pretty display in the orchards. It was to have been a time of plenty, this summer. Was that to be? she wondered.

Onacona accompanied his family for many miles before saying his goodbyes. "I must stand and fight," he told Fiona as he bent to kiss her. "You must fight as well, but in a different way. You must fight to keep our children alive, and my mother and sister, while in the woods. You know how to forage for food, and now is the time when the wild berries are at their best. You know how to hunt and fish, as do all the others. But I warn you, when you reach the deep woods, take our family and go separately from most of the others, for you will be less likely to be found by English patrols if you travel in small groups."

Fiona choked back her tears, and she could barely speak over the tightness in her throat. "I will manage, Onacona, but you must take care of yourself and come back to us." Fiona had developed a keen sense of what Nanyeh called the "spirit vision," what Granny had called "the Sight," and she knew at that moment she would never see him again.

"I will do my best," he replied with a sad smile. "But if for some reason I am taken, either by death or imprisonment, know that my spirit will always abide with you, and in time, we will be joined again in the home of the Great Spirit." With that he looked up at the sky. The day was turning into night, and stars were beginning to show themselves. He pointed to them as he crouched down to say goodbye to his children.

"See the stars," he said. "See how they shine. I want you to shine as brightly. And no matter what happens, whenever you look at the stars, I want you to think of me, the White Owl who loves you."

And with that, he mounted his horse and turned back to Echoe.

* * *

June 24, 1760

In the mountains that lay between the Cherokee Middle and Lower towns, Onacona and a large force of Cherokee warriors positioned themselves high up in a narrow pass south of Echoe and waited. The colonial forces, under the command of Colonel Montgomery, advanced a ranger company which the Indians easily defeated. They took a large toll on the platoons of redcoats that followed, and even some supply wagons, but in the end, those who survived were forced to fall back and take cover in the thick forest.

The following day, despite having incurred heavy casualties, Montgomery led his men on to Echoe, which he found deserted and holding little of value he could claim as loot. Low on supplies and men, the colonel gave up the quest to free Fort Loudoun. They put the village and the surrounding fields and orchards to the torch, then turned around and made their way back to Charlestown.

In their wake, they left more than forty Indians lying dead on the mountainsides. Among them was a fierce and courageous brave named Onacona.

Chapter Thirty-Five

At the headwaters of the Tuckasegee River, North Carolina,
July 1761

The English weren't finished with their determination to wipe out the Cherokee. One year later they returned. And again, Fiona and her family fled their homes at the approach of an avenging and heartless enemy. They had camped at this same site last summer and managed to survive, only to return to find their village almost totally destroyed. She had lost her husband in the battle, and there was no food to be had, since the invaders had burned their crops. She had no reason to believe this year's attack would be any different.

With her in the forest were her children, Aidan and Maura, along with Nanyeh, Alicia and Abe. Unika, Locksley and Arlevia had died over the winter of smallpox, as had many villagers who were weakened from lack of adequate food. Some of the strongest survivors had attempted to rebuild houses and replant fields, but many like herself had chosen to move further north. They'd lived in Nequassee, a larger town than Echoe and one untouched by last year's attack, until news of this latest onslaught drove her back into the safety of the woods. This time, word was the red coats would not stop at Echoe. They intended to destroy all Cherokee Middle Towns.

This night, after she'd quieted the children, she and Alicia slipped away from the campfire and down to the river's edge a few feet away. "What's to become of us?" Alicia asked.

"Maybe we should just jump in the river and get it over with," Fiona replied, not meaning it, but she felt that desperate. Yes, they could survive out here, at least for a time. As Onacona had said, they knew how to live off the land. But what would they do when winter came? And how long would it be until the soldiers came again? If they went back to one of the villages, even if there were some to go back to, how could she stand to endure this again and again until the Cherokee people were no more? How much more terror could her children abide? She called upon her Sight for guidance as to what to do now, but unhappily, nothing came to her.

Wanting to soothe her thoughts, she brought the cane flute out of her battered satchel and began to play a haunting tune she'd learned from the Cherokee. The music summoned Nanyeh and the children from their blankets, and the small band of refugees sat by the river and tried to find some semblance of comfort. Fiona pointed out the stars, and Aidan said, "I see White Owl up there, Mama."

"Yes, he is up there and watching over us," she replied, not believing it for a minute. At the moment, she believed no deity or spirit watched over anyone.

Suddenly Aidan said, "White Owl was not my real Da, was he?"

It was the first time he'd questioned his relationship with Onacona, and Fiona thought hard about how to reply. First, the truth about White Owl. "No, son, he was your adopted father." But before she could continue, and not knowing what she would say next, they all heard a rustle in the woods not far away. Fiona bolted back to the fire and grabbed her rifle. She had little ammunition left, shots she needed to fetch game for food, but she wouldn't hesitate to fire if she saw a red coat. Fire first and ask questions later. Or perhaps this was a bear and would provide food. The others huddled in the shadows and watched.

But it was a man who emerged from the woods and into the light of the fire, a rifle in his hands. He had no red coat, but rather wore the hunting shirt and breeches of a backwoodsman. He was clearly astounded to find himself facing a woman with a gun. Slowly he dropped his own weapon to the ground and raised his hands. "Don't shoot," he said in English.

"Who're you?" Fiona uttered, taking aim at his heart.

"Name's Will. Will Gordon. I won't hurt you."

Fiona's heart was pounding so heavily it sent blood rushing to her ears. "Then leave us," she demanded. She adjusted her stance and raised her head just enough to see him more clearly. He was a tall, lanky fellow with reddish brown hair and light blue eyes. He looked like someone she knew back in Ireland. "You Irish?" she asked.

"Scot," he replied. "A Highlander." And then he greeted her in Gaelic.

Fiona frowned but lowered her gun just a little. "How is it you came upon my camp?"

He grinned. "Heard the sound of a flute."

She swore silently to herself. She hadn't thought of the music giving them away. "So, what are you doing out here anyway? Are you a trader?"

"No. I'm just a farmer out of place," was his simple reply. Something about him diminished Fiona's fear. Maybe it was the Gaelic. Maybe it was his unthreatening manner. He'd not tried to pick up his weapon, nor did he try to approach her further. But he did return her question. "What are you doing out here all alone?"

"I'm not alone," she blurted without thinking. She didn't want him to believe she had no one looking out for her, but she may have betrayed the safety of her children and the others who were in hiding.

He looked around warily but apparently saw no one. "Who are you? This is no country for white women."

She raised her chin defiantly. "This is no country for farmers out of place either, sir. I ask again, why are you here?"

The man lowered his head and took a deep breath. "I rode with the South Carolina militia to invade the Cherokee lands."

Fiona's blood turned cold. "Did you bring them with you? Are we to become your next victims?" she challenged.

"I left them back at Echoe," he told her. "I can't abide what they are doing. I have no fondness for the Cherokee. Some of them killed my wife and some of my family. Neither do I have the appetite for the kind of murder and destruction the English and their colonists have in mind with these raids. I'm on my way back east, to my daughter and friends."

Fiona considered this a moment. Perhaps this was a way out. "Do you know your way?"

"Just following the sun. It always comes up in the east."

"Aren't you afraid? There are still many Indians in these mountains who'd as soon kill you as look at you."

"What about you? You're white. Aren't you afraid of being killed?"

"More afraid of being killed by white men than Indians," she retorted. And then she spoke something in Cherokee, and Maura, holding Nanyeh's hand, emerged from the woods.

"This is my daughter. She is of my Cherokee husband who was killed last summer in the English raid. And my friend, Nanyeh, the child's grandmother."

The man stared at her in open disbelief. "How? Why?"

"'Tis too long of a story, and you are a stranger. I trust no one."

The man hesitated, then looked quizzically at Fiona. "Are you going back to one of those villages? Because I can tell you now, there will be nothing to go back to. Grant and his men are taking anything of value and burning everything else to the ground."

At this Nanyeh let out a small cry and turned her back to the fire. Fiona wanted to drop her gun and go to her, but she feared the intruder would then attack them. She spoke again in Cherokee in a loud voice, and moments later, Alicia and Aidan came into the camp. "Take his gun," Fiona directed Alicia. To Will Gordon she said, "Don't you lay a hand on her."

The man didn't move as Alicia retrieved his gun and aimed it at him. No one spoke for a long moment, then Fiona felt Aidan tug at her skirt.

"Ma," he said in a small voice. "Is he my Da?"

Read Will Gordon's story in Book Two: *Surviving the Now*

Preview

CHAPTER ONE

On board the *Orion*, April 1746

*"**R**un for your life, Will! They've got us!" The words crashed into his ears, along with the sound of guns, the cries of men dying. Sleeting rain pelted his face, and he wanted to run, but he didn't know which way to go. A horrid, metallic smell began to*

pervade the battlefield, the smell of blood mixed with the stench of gunpowder.

"Run for your life!" he heard again and realized it was his friend Duncan who was calling to him. He turned just in time to see Duncan's head blown away. One minute his friend was alive and warning him, the next he was like a piece of raw meat crumpling to the ground.

"Run!" he thought he heard again, but it couldn't be Duncan. Duncan was dead.

Will tried to run, but his feet were mired in the soggy ground of Culloden Muir. He stumbled and fell headlong into the muck. He tried to breathe but was suffocated by the watery ground that oozed around him, even into his nose. He tried to see, but all was suddenly turning dark.

Around him, the screams of the dying filled his ears. He closed his eyes tight, held his breath, clenched his fists, and waited for a bullet or the killing stab of a British bayonet.

Will awoke with a start, bathed in a cold sweat. Would that nightmare ever leave him, the memory of that massacre on the Culloden battlefield that had destroyed his life? Taken his family, his entire clan? He sat up and felt his body being gently rocked in the small bunk where he had slept and remembered where he was…on board a sailing ship, headed away from Scotland and all that he'd ever known.

He rolled over in his tiny bunk, trying to fall asleep again, but his tormented thoughts wouldn't leave him. He remembered regaining consciousness on the sodden moor, how silent it was. The icy rain had stopped. The sky was dark. It was night, and he was alive. He managed to drag himself to his feet and looked around, expecting to see redcoats, but no one was in sight. Shivering, his mind numb, he slogged away from the killing field, not knowing here he was going, only that he had to get away from this place.

Now, as he lay in the dark, remembering that evil day, anger overcame grief, as it always did. He and his Da and all his kinsmen had fought alongside the man who owned their farm, and their lives, Lord Lewis Gordon. But for what? For a royal person he had hardly heard of who some thought should be the English king. Bonnie Prince Charlie, they'd called him. What kind of king had a name like that? And why did Will's kin and clansmen have to die for him? They were Scots, not Englishmen. Will knew his Da was dead, they were all dead. He would be dead too except for the kindness and courage of the couple who'd rescued him in Inverness.

Knowing he could never return to his mother and sisters, or their farm, where redcoats would be watching and would as soon hang him as not, he'd made his way down the mountain to Inverness, taking shelter in an old warehouse. Starving and exhausted, he'd lain across a bundle of shipping sacks, and unable to fight it any longer, fell asleep. A deep voice had startled him awake, and Ian Brodie, another Highlander who hated the British, had taken him home and later arranged passage out of Scotland aboard the *Orion*, the ship that sheltered him now. The captain, John Taylor, had been kind enough as well, but he'd made clear from the outset that Will was to earn his keep like any other of the sailors, despite his young age.

The *Orion* plied the Atlantic between Scotland and America, and much of the westbound cargo included immigrants eager to taste the freedom and prosperity they'd heard would be theirs in the New World. They were to board just such a group at their next port of call on the Isle of Skye, where Captain Taylor's client, Fergus McKinney, tacksman for the Laird of Clan McKinnon, had booked passage for as many of his tenants as wanted to leave. "He told me they're leaving the place before it all turns to shambles," Taylor had shared with Will. "The Laird's already left for London, wanting no part of this current political business, and the tenants canna afford the rents still demanded by the Laird." He paused a moment, then added, "He's a good man, McKinney. Paid shipping for most of 'em. I just hope what the man's heard about America is true. Seems like a wild, unsettled land t' me."

BIBLIOGRAPHY

Alderman, Pat, *The Overmountain Men*, Johnson City, TN: Overmountain Press, 1986.

Bartram, William, *Travels of William Bartram*, edited by Mark Van Doren. New York: Dover Publications, 1955.

Bassett, John Spencer, *The Regulators of North Carolina*, Trinity College, NC, 1894.

Conley, Robert J., *Cherokee Dragon*. Norman, OK: University of Oklahoma Press, 2000.

Dixon, Max, *The Wataugans*. Johnson City, TN: Overmountain Press, 1989.

Duncan, Barbara, collector and editor, *Living Stories of the Cherokee*. Chapel Hill, NC: The University of North Carolina Press, 1998.

Fink, Paul M., "Jacob Brown of Nolichucky." Tennessee Historical Quarterly, Vol. 1. No. 1, Sept. 1962.

Furbee, Mary R., *Wild Rose-Nancy Ward and the Cherokee Nation*. Greensboro, NC: Morgan Reynolds Publishers, Inc., 2002.

Lee, E. Lawrence, *Indian Wars in North Carolina*, 1663-1763. Raleigh, NC: Office of Archives & History, North Carolina Department of Cultural Resources, 2011.

Maas, John R., *The French & Indian War in North Carolina*. Charleston, SC: The History Press, 2013.

McCrumb, Sharyn, *Kings Mountain*, New York: Thomas Dunne Books, St. Martin's Press, 2013.

Mooney, James, *Myths of the Cherokee*. New York: Dover Publications, 1995. (Reprint of Government Printing Office edition, 1900.)

Morgan, Robert, *Boone, A Biography*, Chapel Hill, NC: Algonquin Books of Chapel Hill, 2008.

Ritchie, Fiona, and Doug Orr, *Wayfaring Strangers-The Musical Voyage from Scotland and Ulster to Appalachia*. Chapel Hill, NC: The University of North Carolina Press, 2014.

Shames, Susan P., *The Old Plantation-The Artist Revealed*. Williamsburg, VA: The Colonial Williamsburg Foundation, 2010.

Swann, Anne Landis, *The Other Side of the River*. Kearney, NE: Morris Publishing, 2010.

Swisher, James K., *The Revolutionary War in the Southern Back Country*. Gretna, LA: Pelican Publishing Company, 2008.

The Junior League of Charleston, Inc., *Charleston Receipts*. Memphis, TN: Starr Toof Cookbook Division, 1950.

Timberlake, Henry, *Memoirs*. Signal Mountain, TN: Mountain Press, 2001 (reprint of original work, 1762.)

Woodward, Grace Steele, *The Cherokees*. Norman, OK: University of Oklahoma Press, 1963.

www.ingramcontent.com/pod-product-compliance
Lightning Source LLC
Chambersburg PA
CBHW020148120726
47903CB00007B/2460